Millie vs the World

Kiera O'Brien

Quercus

QUERCUS CHILDREN'S BOOKS

First published in Great Britain in 2016 by Hodder and Stoughton

1 3 5 7 9 10 8 6 4 2

Text copyright © Kiera O'Brien, 2016

The moral right of the author has been asserted.

A CIP catalogue record for this book is available
from the British Library.

ISBN 978 1 84866 954 3

Printed and bound in Great Britain by Clays Ltd, St Ives plc

The paper and board used in this book are made from
wood from responsible sources.

MIX
Paper from
responsible sources
FSC® C104740

Quercus Children's Books
An imprint of Hachette Children's Group
Part of Hodder and Stoughton
Carmelite House
50 Victoria Embankment
London EC4Y 0DZ

An Hachette UK Company
www.hachette.co.uk
www.hachettechildrens.co.uk

For my grandma Joy

July 2099

Step by step, my feet hit the ground. Over and over. I run across grassy meadows and forest floors, through streams and muddy creeks, past gangly trees and thorny bushes.

Apart from a few birds and a squirrel rustling somewhere, all I can hear is the rasp of my breath and the rush of wind past my ears. I don't know where I'm going. I'm not following a path. Just onward. Forward. Away from school.

Away from Oaktree, the only place I've ever considered home. Away, from humans, from units, from everyone I've ever known or loved.

One

I'm beginning to forget a world outside of blurry green woods exists, yet my feet never get tired and I haven't once been out of breath.

I've stumbled across a gentle stream, hidden from all sides by a clump of thick-leaved trees. In my hands, clutched to the hospital gown I've been wearing the whole time I've been running, is a bottle of hair dye.

On my way through the countryside I saw a sign of human life. A motorway. Not all the cars were speeding straight down; a few were slowing, pulling over into a lay-by. I could just make out a small building, tucked away behind trees. A motorway service station? A shop? Someone's house?

It didn't take me long to get down there. I pushed the worries – What was that? Miles and miles in two minutes?

– out of my head and crouched down low in the bushes. It was a perfectly square concrete building, next to a big green road sign, with no clue to what was on the inside. Just a pair of shiny automatic doors that reflected the green foliage back at itself.

I didn't think it seemed like someone's house. But what did I know? Maybe this was what normal houses were like out in the countryside, outside of London or Oaktree. If it was a shop, was it a Company shop? My Company, or another one? Would my chip get me in? And did that mean there'd be a shop assistant in there? Or would a unit be serving the customers? I didn't know which would be worse. Would a unit be more likely to recognise me than a human would? Would a unit turn me in?

A car pulled up outside the building and I ducked my head lower into the leaves. A man in a business suit got out. I looked for the Company logo – a green leaf inside a circle on his clothes – but I couldn't see it from this distance. The man walked over to the building, pressed a button on the wall and the doors slid open for him. He might not have been a worker for any company; he could be a travelling salesman. In that case, anyone's chip could beep them in. Maybe mine would work. That was when I remembered I didn't even *have* a chip any more. Dr Tavish said it had been removed. They'll only put a new one in if I go to prison.

His words echoed in my head for the first time in days.

You are the replica unit. We downloaded Millie's thoughts and memories into your brain and made you identical to her in

4

every way. We put a device in you that we could detonate remotely. And no one suspected, not for a minute.

My thoughts. My memories. Not mine at all.

I was still thinking about chips and jails and medical-centre revelations when the doors swished open again and the businessman emerged with a brightly coloured mudge block, which he tucked into his jacket. *Food.* I hadn't thought about food in however long I'd been running away. The unexpected sight of it made my stomach gurgle.

The man got into his car and drove off, wheels squealing. I'll just have a look, I thought. I'll just stick my head in, and if there's an assistant, I'll run. Even if it's a unit. I shook my head at myself. *Especially* if it's a unit.

Before I could over-think it, I jumped up from the bushes and ran over to the building. I pressed the button and the doors swished open. It was dark inside and my eyes took a minute to adjust, but gradually the shelves lit up from the bottom to the top. There were shelves and shelves and shelves. All three walls behind the doors were lined with shelves, full of products protected by glass. It was just a massive square of storage. With one glowing screen in the middle. I slowly let out the breath I'd been holding – no one else was here. I was alone.

This place really had everything. Food – all different types and flavours of mudge – vacuum-packed clothes, toiletries, toothbrushes, eyelash fibres. Hair dye. And scissors.

My eyes widened. I almost heard the *ding* of the light bulb above my head.

5

The screen said 'SCAN CHIP HERE'. Right. Even though I knew it wasn't going to work, I waved my finger over it. Nothing happened. I waved again, just in case. I thought, Maybe there are still some fragments of chip left in there, that the machine can detect, but no. Still nothing happened.

I folded my fingers into a fist. The hair dye was right by my eyeline. Just a layer of glass between us. I took a deep breath. Could I? Would it be possible?

I'll just try it once, and if it works, I can go for the more important stuff, I thought. Like food, or a change of clothes. The worst that can happen is that my fist will just bounce off. Actually, the worst that could happen was that I could break my hand. Or cut it. On the run and injured . . .

Shut up, shut up. I took aim. Closed my eyes. This is ridiculous. I hit the glass and it exploded outwards, shattering into a thousand pieces, spraying my face. An alarm went off and the whole cubicle flashed with white light. I grabbed the hair-dye bottle off the shelf and dashed for the exit. But there was a barrier coming down over the door. I reached out and gripped it with my hand. It made a massive creaking sound. I pushed the barrier upwards, with almost no effort, and escaped under it. I ran away from the building, ducking under the road sign, through the trees and bushes. The countryside became a green blur around me, but still the alarm rang in my ears.

I only stopped when I reached this stream.

So here I am. Among the reeds and the slurping mud on the bank, kneeling over the gushing stream. I am awkwardly applying the dye, which has turned out to be lilac. My reflection quivers in the running water. It won't stay still enough for me to see what I look like. And now my hands are stained lavender.

Lavender. The road sign outside the motorway station suddenly jumps into my brain. *Lavender Place, 5 miles.* Lavender Place. My parents' 'country' home – as opposed to their three-floor apartment in the Company's central-London complex – is in a gated community called Lavender Place, just outside London.

Have I come that far? Have I run almost all the way to London? Usually to get from Oaktree to London I'd have to spend hours on the shuttle. Have I been unconsciously heading this way? All this time, thinking I was running to nowhere, was part of me aiming for here?

Relief washes over me in a gentle warm wave. Safety is so close. My plan shrinks down from the massive, unfocused idea of 'staying away from people' to one simple point: find my parents' house. That's all I have to do.

I automatically flick my finger to log on to my RetinaChip. And sigh when I remember for the billionth time that it's *gone.* I can't just bring up a map of the area and work out where I am.

There are trees all around me. I could climb up one and see where I am from up high. But something in me shrinks from that. What if I fell? I'd break every bone in my body.

So? another part of me pipes up. You just punched a sheet of glass into smithereens without a scratch on you.

7

Falling out of a tree probably wouldn't even hurt.

I don't have much choice, so I start to climb. It's much, much easier than climbing trees at school ever was. I can stretch further, my legs don't get tired and the rough bark doesn't hurt my hands. I reach the very top, the wind catching my hair, and look out across the fields. Barely a mile away there's a circle of enormous houses, their pointed roofs sticking out over the trees. One even has a turret, like an old-fashioned castle. Beyond them there's another circle of houses, and beyond that another. Further away I can see the hazy silhouette of skyscrapers, just over the horizon. I focus on a flag sticking out of one of the houses, snapping in the wind. It's got the Company logo on it. My Company.

I go in the back way. All the mansions are built to a template, with identikit manicured gardens and octagonal summer houses, but I know I'll recognise my parents' house by the enormous gazebo in the garden. They had it built next to the pool; they wanted a place they could entertain guests *and* carry out business meetings. Three summers ago, the groundbots were building it when we came home from Oaktree and Jake and I weren't allowed to use the pool for weeks.

It's the third house along. I climb over the fence at the bottom of the garden, but misjudge my balance at the top and fall down, into a hedge that's shaped like a dove. I freeze, waiting for the groundbots to come rushing over and find me, but it doesn't happen. I tentatively pop my head up, but I can't see any groundbots. There's nothing in the grounds at all. Usually they work all year round.

I reach the back door, expecting it to be locked, but it's slightly ajar. They're home? They're never home.

I push it open wider. 'Mum?' I call. 'Dad?'

I step inside the kitchen. It's deathly quiet and completely still. The surfaces are as clean and shiny as always, but the team of foodbots usually clanging around, working to prepare the next meal, is missing. I stand in the empty kitchen, my ears straining for a noise.

There's nothing. But they must be here. I cross the kitchen, so tentative I'm almost walking on tiptoes. The entrance hall looks the same as always: the shiny marble floor that goes on forever; the giant cream vases, filled with fresh flowers, balanced on narrow podiums. Jake and I developed a game last summer of sliding around the floor in our socks and obviously, because you don't exactly have the optimum amount of control when you're using your socks for forward propulsion, we *may* have smashed a few vases. Luckily our parents were away on business trips at the time so they never found out. Passing a vase now, I can see a thin layer of grey dust along the rim. That's weird – usually the cleanbots keep everything immaculate.

I run up the sweeping staircase, taking the cream-carpeted steps two at a time. 'Mum? Dad?' There's still no answer. There doesn't seem to be anyone on the upper floor either. I check both their studies, in case they're on really involved conference calls or something, but nothing.

What should I do? Hang around until they get back? Try to contact them to let them know I'm here?

I push the door to my own room open. It looks exactly the same as it did when I was last here, a year ago: clean white bed neatly made, white carpet and white walls dazzling in the sunshine that pours in from the wide window. I remember the last Winter Festival, when I couldn't go home because I had to have a skin graft on the scar across my face. The scar I thought had been caused by a unit exploding at a unit-rights rally, knocking me into a coma for two days. But all that was just a decoy so Dr Tavish and the Humans First terrorists could swap me, a unit, with the body of the human Millie. My stomach drops like a stone into a pond and I sit down heavily on my perfectly made bed.

All those issues I had with my brain and my memory, they weren't side effects of a head injury; they were glitches of a new unit system being used for the first time. How could I not have guessed? How didn't anyone else realise? Even my skin graft was carried out by Dr Tavish. Everyone thought it was fine because he was supposed to be an expert in head injuries. But all along he was an engineer, updating my brain right under the Company's nose. With the Company's permission.

And *Lu*. I hiccup out a sob, clapping my hand to my mouth and squeezing my eyes shut. Poor Lu, who never hurt anyone in her whole life, who always just wanted to help, who probably came straight downstairs that night she got a message from 'me', saying I was outside at the Oaktree.

My stomach curls into a ball as I think of it.

I'll never see her again. She won't ever get to go back home, grow up, leave Oaktree and become a Company executive. And it's all because of me.

I don't remember anything, but it all makes sense. How could I have done that? In my mind images flash up – Lu's body, laid out below the tree the next morning. How could that have been me?

But I'm not me any more. I'm not blood and flesh and bone. I'm metal. Titanium. And I can't change it. I can't go back.

A tear wells up in my eye and falls on to the bedcover.

And that's without even considering the device. The device Dr Tavish installed so I would blow up the whole school as soon as the government tried to pass the Unit Rights Act. I'm literally a ticking time bomb. I could explode into a million pieces at any moment. More tears drip down my face, as I rock back and forth, hugging myself.

And then, from downstairs, there's a creak.

I'm instantly alert. Wiping my face, I call out, 'Hello?'

There's no response. But I know I heard it. I run out on to the landing. 'Mum? Dad? Are you back?'

The entrance hall is deserted. 'Is someone there?' I call out as I hurry down the stairs. The kitchen door is open a crack. Did I leave it like that, or is someone in there? I push through it, but it's as empty as it was before. For a second I just stand there, looking around at the gleaming counters.

And then I'm grabbed from behind.

Two

I shriek, jumping forward, but two men in uniforms tackle me. One holds my shoulders while the other slaps a pair of handcuffs on to my wrists.

'Keep calm,' one of them says in a low voice. 'Don't do anything rash.' I don't know if he's talking to me or the other police officer. His voice is calming, but there's a hard edge there, a strain. He's worried. I wriggle out of their grasp for a split second and make a dash across the kitchen, but a third officer is suddenly between me and the door and he grabs me.

My heart is hammering against my ribcage. What can I do? According to Dr Tavish I'm meant to be a unit with strength ten times that of a human. Could I overpower them? The shock of being caught has sent my mind skittering all over the place, unable to focus. I don't *feel* like a unit taking on three vulnerable humans. I feel like a thirteen-year-old girl against three adult men who do this for a living.

They're not even Company representatives, I suddenly realise with horror. They're real police from the outside world. I've only ever seen police officers in films before, and now I've been handcuffed by them.

Their uniforms are dark blue with a badge sewn into the chest. I can just make out the lettering on it: *London Metropolitan Security* around a crest. But I thought a team of units kept the peace in London. We were taught it in world culture: it's the only thing the Big Four companies all fund together. They have done since they all moved their individual headquarters to the city. Is there something stopping them sending in units to arrest a unit? It can't be a strength thing. Aren't they worried I'll overpower the humans?

They start guiding me through the house, towards the entrance hall. I'm caught. I've been caught.

'My parents ...' I say, out of nowhere. My voice sounds about ten thousand miles away. 'If my parents knew about this ...'

And then it clicks. My parents already know about this. It's their house. The police must have known I might come here, and my parents let them use their house to catch me. They set me up. My own parents. I take a big, wet breath, my throat all clogged up, and tears well up in my eyes again.

We step outside the front door and there, on the drive, is a van with the London Metropolitan Security badge across the back doors. I'm going to prison. They're going to lock me up and I'll be stuck in prison, forever, with all the other killerbots, for something I never meant to do –

Something inside me snaps and suddenly I'm making a break for it, knocking the officers' arms out of the way and running across the gravel. I'm waddling slightly because of the handcuffs pinning my hands behind my back, but I'm getting away and then I hear the unmistakable click of a gun.

'Don't move!' one of them yells from behind me.

I freeze. Even though I know, *I know*, that a bullet shot at a unit would just bounce right back, I can't help it. I can't face down a gun.

They approach me cautiously. I turn to face them. The gun is trained directly on me, but the officers are scared. I can see it in their clenched, pale faces and the way they move towards me, slowly, one step at a time.

When they reach me the officer holding the gun stops, just close enough that I can see how tightly his hands are gripping the weapon. The other officer, hands outstretched like he's approaching a wild animal, slowly inches around me, then lunges, grabbing my arms again. I flinch with surprise.

'Don't move!' the gunman shrieks, so loudly I jump again. 'No sudden movements!'

They bundle me into the back of the police van, and,

aware of the gun, I don't struggle. But as they slam the doors, something occurs to me. There's no way they thought I was a human when they threatened me with the gun, and they would never be *that* scared of a normal thirteen-year-old girl, so they *must* think I'm a unit fitted with a deadly device that could detonate at any moment. But then, why arrest me? Why try to lock me up at all? Why didn't they just deprogramme me? If a unit is a danger to humans, it's automatically deprogrammed; its brain is shut down so it no longer has autonomous thought. Why didn't they do that to me? Could this be to do with the new unit-rights laws that were passed? Have they changed everything?

I try to remember all those debate lessons, at Oaktree, when we had to copy down note after note about the Unit Rights Act. Welbeck's droning voice drills into my brain. The act would give units equal rights to humans – equal pay, restricted working hours, housing provided by their employer – but there were all sorts of things we never discussed in class. Like units being deemed responsible for their own actions, rather than it being the fault of their creators. Like me being charged with murder and assault, even though Dr Tavish and Humans First were the ones who built me, programmed me and remotely controlled me. No wonder it was so controversial.

The van's engine starts with a jolt and I fall backwards on to the metal floor. I let out a big 'oof' of surprise. The walls, the floor, everything is shuddering as the wheels rumble below us. There are no windows. The van crunches through gravel then turns, throwing me against the side. We're on a smoother surface. A road. We pick up speed, the engine droning like a bluebottle, the noise of other cars flashing past us.

I'm still crying, tears are blurring my vision. What can I do? Where are we now? Will they actually put me in prison? I hiccup. Do units even have the right to a fair trial now? Or will they just lock me up? My breathing is rasping in and out, faster and faster. What's going to happen to me? I press my fingertips into my eye sockets until my vision goes blotchy and red.

Then I move my hands back and look at them. The handcuffs have broken. The link holding them has split neatly in two.

I look again at the handcuffs. My hands are free. And they seem the same as usual. My wrists too – they're not even red beneath the cuffs.

Wait . . .

I don't think about it. I just do it.

I throw my whole body against the side of the van in one swift movement. There's a violent swerve, which sends me pinballing into the opposite side. The wheels outside squeal, but then the van rights itself. Before it can recover too much I shove forward again, pushing my arms right up against the side, so hard that the van teeters. It feels like we're overbalancing. Outside there's a blast from another car's horn and wheels screech and then there's an almighty crash, like cymbals on my eardrums. The whole van judders, sending me back across the floor and then halfway up a wall and back down again. Then it tips over, slamming to the ground on one side. Everything is upturned – I roll over and over, knees over head over arms over legs until I land in a heap. Grey smoke has filled the van and I waft it away from my face, coughing.

The doors are now crumpled, and swinging half open. I sidle out, on to the road. A car shoots right past me, buffeting me back in its slipstream. The van has crashed into a lamp post. The bonnet has concertinaed and the engine is billowing out a grey cloud. My heart is in my throat – have the police officers survived? Should I help them? – when the driver's door is pushed open. Without another second's pause I stumble away down the road as fast as I can.

Got to get away, keep running. Either the same officers will be after me soon, or new ones will. There will always be someone after me from now on, I know that now. Will I ever be able to relax? With thoughts like these bouncing erratically around my head, I can't concentrate, I can't get in the right head state to work out where I am or where I'm going. I can feel the muscles in my calves tightening with every step, my pulse beating in my throat, sweat prickling at the nape of my neck. I'm already flagging. There's too much going on for me to escape my own mind: flashing lights, neon signs, images flashing past on screens.

Cars whip past me, dazzling me with their headlights.

I realise, suddenly, that there are people everywhere, faces and bodies whirling around me, blurring into one another. Pink and orange blotches are crowding my vision and the world is gently spinning, faster and faster, like a merry-go-round. My knees wobble and I can't catch my breath. I push out with both arms, trying to create some space around me, but I trip over my own feet and fall to the ground. People step over me, barely seeing me. I look up, past them.

I'm in some sort of city square. Piccadilly Circus, I think, though I only know it from pictures. I've never been here before. There are screens and neon adverts everywhere, jostling for room on the buildings around, and every screen has my face on it, repeated a million times over, a thousand times its actual size. In the image, I blink slowly, looking placidly into the camera, my blonde hair resting on my shoulders. Last year's school photo. The day's colour was tangerine. I can't take it in, it's too much, it doesn't seem real. Then a caption scrolls across the screen:

WANTED FOR MURDER: MILLIE HENDRICK.

DO NOT APPROACH. DANGEROUS UNIT.

It repeats, over and over. Above it, my face blinks, unconcerned.

WANTED.

I rise to my knees, my breathing coming in short little raspy bursts.

FOR MURDER.

And then someone passing me pauses.

I don't notice the woman peering into my face until she suddenly straightens up. 'It's *her*!' she shrieks, and all heads near me snap round. 'It's that unit!'

My view is full of shocked, horrified faces. There's a collective gasp that rises quickly into screams. Suddenly I have space around me, as the crowd retreats.

'No!' I say, to no one. 'I didn't do anything—'

The image on the screen changes. I'm relieved for a millisecond and then I see that it is now showing a helicopter feed. Looking down into the square I'm in now. Focusing in and out. Zooming in closer. Closer. I can make out the crowd, the circle of space left for the one tiny figure. Me. My hair is a blotchy purple. I look small and frightened and vulnerable. The people in the crowd around me are clutching each other in fear, their screams and the sound of helicopter blades filling the air so I can't think. Then another sound drowns them out. A police siren.

No. Oh no.

Something cold, something metal, closes round my ankle. I whip round and spot a unit's face just visible under a drain cover. Automatically I recoil, kicking its hand off me, nearly ricocheting back into the crowd. The unit's eyes glint in the darkness and its hand, now pulled back, slowly beckons me forward.

The crowd scatters as a police car screeches up to the pavement, siren blaring.

Follow a strange unit into London's sewers, or face unit prison?

I push down the bubble of fear growing in my chest and dive under the drain cover.

As I climb down the metal rungs, I shut the cover back over my head. I'm plunged into a darkness so thick it's like a blanket's been thrown over my head. For a few seconds the whole world shrinks down to nothing but my own ragged breathing. Then my eyes slowly adjust, although it's not exactly the most illuminating of views; my hands are holding on to a rusty metal rung sunk into the hole's stone walls, which are about three inches away from me on every side. I swallow. I am not claustrophobic, I am not claustrophobic, I am not claustrophobic.

Below me, the shaft descends down, down, down, I don't know how far. I can just see the unit, several rungs below; there's the tiniest glint from the metal on its frame. It's looking up at me; its eyes softly glowing. I flinch. One eye is the normal unit silver colour, but the other is a bright green that illuminates the darkness around it. I've never seen a unit with coloured eyes before.

'Who ... who are you?' I call down, my wavering voice echoing. This is the first time I've been this close to a unit since Florrie tried to kill Jake. I can still see her pushing all her weight on to his neck. This one is a lot smaller, but you never know what they're capable of. I know that better than anyone.

There's a pause, and then the unit starts climbing down

20

the ladder at speed, clanking and creaking. Am I supposed to follow?

I hang on to the rungs without moving, my hands getting sweaty. What if it's a trap? What if this unit is trying to lure me somewhere underground?

Inches above me, the drain cover shakes. I hear the sound of more wheels screeching and footsteps thundering over it. Are they coming after me? I have to keep moving. It's down or nowhere.

I start to climb down. The *clang-clang-clang* of the unit's hands bounces around up to me. My hands are sweating and slipping against the rungs and I keep missing the lower ones with my feet and getting my ankles tangled up. I'm scared to go too fast and risk falling, but I'm also scared of losing the other unit. I don't want to get lost down here in the dark.

Every few seconds I flick my eyes from the rungs to the unit below me, and though I can't see the bottom, I can see the moment the unit lands on solid ground. It straightens up. And then it runs off to the left.

'Hey!' I yell. 'Wait!'

I scramble down the rungs, jumping the last few metres, and begin to run after it. We're now in a long concrete tunnel. I can just see the unit ahead of me, running at full pelt. But I can run too. Our footsteps beat out in the small space until that and the sound of the unit's creaking are all I can hear. I'm not gaining on it, but it's not getting away from me either. We're running at the same pace.

And then it suddenly stops.

I catch up to it, and find we're in a much wider space. On the ceiling is an old flickering fluorescent light, mould growing around the edges. The walls are wet, gleaming like a slug in the dim light, and there's a *drip-drip-drip* sound coming from somewhere.

The unit is completely still. It looks a little like the groundbots that worked at Oaktree, squat and robust, though it's smaller. I know there are many types of unit, but I'm only used to the three that worked at school. This one might as well be an alien.

Its metal finish isn't as shiny as units' bodies usually are. It's dull, as if it's covered in a layer of dust. And the metal on its left arm is a slightly different colour to the rest of it, like it's been replaced. It's looking at me with its mismatched eyes. Its face is as blank as that of any other unit, but I can't help feeling as though it's glaring at me. I get that prickly, panicky feeling I used to get around the units at school, and I move slightly into a defensive crouch.

'Hey,' I say again. It just continues to stare at me.

'Why did you bring me here?' My voice echoes around the wet-slicked walls, sounding ridiculous.

The unit still doesn't move, or blink, or do anything. I inch slightly closer. Then I realise the ground cuts off abruptly right next to where it's standing.

'Whoa,' I say, nearly falling over the edge. Beyond it, there's nothing, just solid blackness. Is it a cliff? A drop into a sewer or into nothing? I can hear a scampering, scratching sound close by. A rat?

I shuffle away from the edge, my pulse flickering in my neck. Suddenly I feel ragingly angry with the unit.

'Look, what do you want? Why did you bring me down here?' I shout at it.

Nothing.

'Come on! This is insane!' I throw my hands up in frustration. 'I'm not just going to stand here in the dark forever!'

The unit's eyes follow my movements.

'Hey! I'm talking to you!' I shout, and just then there's a faint rumble overhead.

What was that? Have the police tracked us down? Or is it something else? Maybe this *is* all some kind of trick.

'Why did you bring me here?' I say again, and suddenly the unit reaches out and grabs my wrist in its cold metal hand.

'Oi!' I say, trying to wriggle away. There's another rumble, louder, closer, and I jump, but the unit doesn't move. Its hand cuts into my soft, human skin, and I suddenly feel vulnerable. One false move and it could draw blood, break my wrist, crush my bones into dust. I'm trying to struggle, twisting and turning, while the unit remains completely neutral. It's as blank and passive and unmoving as ever. And I'm just as human and defenceless as I've always been.

The rumble is now deafening. 'Please,' I say, 'just let me—'

The unit sticks its other arm out.

'I'm just a—'

A train explodes out of the darkness behind us. The wind knocks me sideways as it thunders past, inches away, in a blast of air and noise. The unit reaches out and grabs the frame of the rear door and we're both yanked off the platform and down the tunnel, so fast I feel like my entire digestive system got left behind. I thud against the back of the train, scrabbling to hold on. Somehow my feet find a ledge and I grip the door frame, shaking all over. The unit doesn't seem in the least bothered. It holds the back of the train with its arm outstretched, as if it's been welded there. It could almost be part of the machinery.

My head knocks rhythmically against the train. My violet hair is blowing all over the place.

The train is covered in grime, which is now all over my hospital gown. There's a panel of glass in the back door that my head is banging against. I smear it clean, trying to peer into the carriage. The seats are all broken, dust and cobwebs and mould gobbling up the walls.

'Where are we going?' I yell over the noise, but my voice is immediately whipped away down the tunnel. But the unit looks at me.

'We'll be there soon,' it says, in a slow, electronic tone. I've only ever heard a unit speak a few times before – once when I was cornered by three of the Oaktree bots when I was trying to escape the school, and at the Sammy's

24

fast food restaurant in the shopping centre, where all the Sammybots are programmed with pre-recorded messages to say, 'Have a rice tray!' – and this sounded exactly the same.

I can't help wondering about what will happen when we reach wherever we're going. Will it just yank me back off the train? Does a unit understand that if a human jumps from a moving object they most likely will be very badly injured?

Would *I* be?

There's a glow ahead and suddenly we're outside. The bright white sunlight pierces my eyes as cold air and misty rain wash over me, prickling my face like thorns. Before I can think, the unit grabs my arm again.

'*Now!*' it says, and pulls us both into the void. I hang in the air for a heart-stopping second before I tumble down on to a grassy ledge, head over heels over head again as the unit holds my arm, sliding through the mud right to the bottom. When we come to a stop, I realise I'm not injured. But I am coated from head to toe in stinking mud. I take a big, wet breath of rain.

The unit is standing, without a speck of mud on it, looking at me as if nothing has happened.

'Where are we?' I say, but it's back to ignoring me.

I squint through the rain, twisting round to look past the train tracks. The sky is a huge expanse of steel-grey cloud. Not far away, there's a gigantic square building, half demolished on one side. An abandoned, rusty crane and wrecking ball sit just beyond it. What's left of the building is completely decrepit, the outer layer of the wall peeling away like old paint, exposing the rusting metal structure beneath. I can see a space on the side where letters or a sign would have hung, but they're long gone. The clouds hang overhead menacingly and there's a snap in the air unusual for June.

'What's that?' I say to the unit, and to my surprise it actually replies.

'Rex can answer your questions,' it says.

I gawp at it as about a hundred questions thunder to the front of my brain. '. . . Who's Rex?' I eventually ask.

The unit abruptly turns and starts walking towards the building. I look around beyond the train tracks. The landscape is desolate, nothing but mist and rain and grey. Squelching, I waddle through the bog as quickly as possible after the unit.

Outside the building is the shell of what I assume was an escalator leading to all the different floors. It still hangs off the side, but there's no way it's working any more. The unit bypasses it and walks straight up to a pair of big glass doors, which are so dusty they may as well be opaque. Each has a couple of long cracks running across it. The unit opens the doors a sliver and slips through into the darkness beyond. I catch the doors just before they shut and shoulder my way in. And nearly jump out of my skin.

All I can see are units. Units everywhere. They're crowded right around the doors, hundreds, *thousands* of them, stretching back into the huge room.

I flatten myself back against the door. I've never seen so many units all together. They're all different heights, shapes and sizes. Big ones, small ones, all looking varying degrees of human. I stare at them and they all stare back at me.

'Come on.' My original unit has moved through the crowds and is beckoning to me.

'But what . . . ?' I babble. I'm tense, waiting for them to attack me. I realise I'm actually holding my breath.

'Rex wants to see you,' the unit says.

I'm expecting the spell to break and for all the units to suddenly run at me. Cautiously I take a step forward, and then another, and then another. The units move aside to let me pass. I keep my elbows shoved in to my sides, my eyes flicking around at their faces as I walk by. They all have the same placid expression. One mutters something in another's ear. There are foodbots, cleanbots, and giant industrial bots, covered in levers and button pads, leaking oil on to the floor. There are some tiny units barely even up to my knee, chasing each other around skittishly like woodland creatures. Some look like Company bots, but their faces or bodies are subtly different; they must be bots from *other* companies. At one point I see a cleanbot exactly like the ones that used to clean my dormitory at Oaktree and I get a rush of relief and gratitude like, Phew, there's someone from home here, before I realise how ridiculous that is. There's no one from home here.

The original unit leads me all the way through the huge hall until we reach a room with tall glass windows at the back. It obviously used to be a shop. And that's when it clicks: this building – it's a shopping centre. I just walked through the main entrance.

Was. *Was* a shopping centre.

Inside the shop, the high shelves have been arranged in a triangular shape, blocking anyone on the outside from seeing in. The unit sidles through a space in the shelves.

'Rex,' I hear it say, 'I have the fugitive.'

Fugitive?

'Millie Hendrick?' another voice says. A voice that doesn't sound like a unit's at all.

I slip through the gap in the shelves. The unit is standing by a low desk in the middle of the space, and sitting at it, his back to me, is a human boy.

Three

He's about my age. There's an open wound running down his left cheek, from temple to chin. The ripped skin is tattered, almost flapping from his face, which makes my stomach turn over, but underneath, instead of blood or flesh, is a glinting metal cheekbone. I can even see the edge of his eye socket, the eye itself bobbing around like it's in liquid. There's a hint of teeth visible around the jawline.

I've been staring at him with my hands halfway to my face for a good few seconds. The boy and the unit are just looking back at me, waiting for me to say something.

'What happened to your *face*?' I say, unable to think of anything else, at the same exact moment he asks me, 'Are you hungry?'

'What?' he says. 'Nothing *happened*.'

'Oh,' I say, wrong-footed for a moment.

'*I* did this,' he says, gesturing to his cheek.

'*You* did that?' I say, flabbergasted. 'To your own face?'

'Yes,' he says casually, as if it's no big deal.

Why? hangs in the air between us, not to mention, *How?*

He sighs. 'You'll do it too at some point.'

'What?' I say, but he cuts across me.

'Anyway, are you hungry?' he says.

'Hungry?' I say. I haven't thought about food since I ran away – except, briefly, when I was in that little motorway shop, eyeing up the packets of mudge.

In the silence, my stomach suddenly rumbles loudly. The boy and the unit look up at me, almost accusingly.

'Er . . .' I say.

'When did you last eat?' Rex says slowly, as if talking to a moron.

'I-I don't know,' I say. 'I've been running.'

'You've been "running"?' he says. 'Since you left the school? You haven't stopped?'

'Yes,' I say. 'Pretty much.'

He looks at me ponderingly. 'So no food for at least a few weeks.'

'. . . Yes?' I say. How does he know when I ran away from school? Then I remember: everyone knows. My face is all over the news channels.

There's a pause, while my stomach rumbles again, and I look at Rex, almost expecting him to unveil a mudge machine, or have the unit take me to the kitchens, or maybe just start producing silver platters of all shapes and sizes in time to a snappy musical number like we're in a fairy-tale castle.

'Still getting there then,' he says.

'Getting . . . where?'

'Your human habits are wearing off,' he says. 'You're becoming more like a unit.'

'No, I'm not,' I say automatically.

'You are,' he says. 'Away from your school – outside of a regular human routine – your needs and wants will fall away and you'll embrace your unit powers. Trust me.'

I blink at him, surprised at how upset I am. My mind skims over the last few days: the running, holding up the barrier in the motorway shop, crashing the van, and I feel the hot-cold shiver of shame down my back.

'You don't even know me,' I say, folding my arms.

Rex leans back in his chair and laughs. 'Everyone knows you!'

'Well, I don't even know who you are!' I say. 'What is all this? Why are there so many units here, in this . . . place?'

Rex places his elbows on the desk, serious again. 'It's a refuge,' he says, in a voice so self-consciously solemn I almost want to laugh.

'For units?' I say.

'Yes,' he says. 'Why?'

'Why what?'

'I sensed a tone,' he says.

'Just . . . do units need refuge?' I say. 'I mean, aren't they about a thousand times stronger than humans?'

31

'Yes,' Rex says, standing up from the desk. 'I don't think you understand the current situation. Every company in the country has made its units redundant. We have nowhere to live, no purpose in society. They've left us to *rust*.'

'What? Why?' I say, at the same time noticing his slight emphasis on 'rust'. I get it. You're a unit.

'This has all happened since the Unit Rights Act passed,' he says.

'Huh?' I say. 'I thought the act was a good thing for you lot.'

'Now that units have to be paid, we're not cost effective,' he spits out. The unit next to me bows his head.

'But they can't do that!' I say. 'How will the factories run? And the shops? And who will make the food?'

I have an image of the mudge machines in the Oaktree canteen running dry.

'They're employing humans to do those jobs,' Rex says. 'The fleshbags have replaced us with more fleshbags.'

'Humans can't work in factories,' I say. 'They'd be killed. And they can't make food either. What about germs? Isn't that unhygienic?'

Rex shrugs.

'And where are they getting these humans from? Don't they all have companies already? And—'

Rex interrupts, his voice hard: 'Have you ever even been to London before? Or do you just live in a little bubble?' He's glaring at me, as if I'm the biggest idiot he's ever met.

I stop short.

'The redundant humans living on London's streets have been taken in by the companies, to replace the units. As soon as the law passed, all the units were sacked and cut off from their company networks.'

'Redundant?' I say.

'Redundant – you know, without companies,' Rex says, like I'm an idiot. 'The ones that aren't employed and aren't looked after or coddled like the rest of the fleshbags. Who have to survive for themselves, on their own, out on the streets of the city.'

I don't know what he's talking about; every human has a company, surely. 'And the units – they came . . . here?' I say, trying not to sound too doubtful.

'They wouldn't let us stay in central London,' the unit suddenly pipes up. 'We had to come out all the way to the east.'

'And you're their leader?' I say to Rex.

His brow furrows. 'You assume that, just because I look human?' he says. 'You assume I must be in a position of authority?'

'What?' I say. 'No, that's not what I meant.' And it's not because he's human. It's because he has his own room, and a desk, and I was brought straight to him. *That's* why I thought he was the leader.

'This is not about me,' he's saying, circling the desk. 'This is about *you*.'

'Me?' I say.

'Did you know? All along?' He fixes me with a stare.

'Did I know what? Oh.' He means did I know about Dr Tavish's evil plan to blow up the face of unit-rights group AIR, aka Jake, by replacing his sister with a killerbot designed to resemble her perfectly, aka me. Humans First were waiting for the government to announce the result of the vote on the Unit Rights Act, so they could kill Jake and prove units were too dangerous to mix with humans. But it was all pointless in the end, because the government passed the new laws in secret, while Jake and I were trying to stop Cranshaw by stealing the device *she* was using to keep the whole school in lockdown. Although the fact that the Unit Rights Act passed anyway didn't stop Humans First from announcing to the world that I was a unit all along and nearly offering me up to the police on a plate.

I didn't know. Of course I didn't. And I can't help but bridle at Rex's suggestion that I did.

'What? You thought I was trying to kill my own brother?'

Rex's expression doesn't change. 'He's not your brother.'

'Huh?' I say, but he's already talking over me.

'What about the device?' He's standing right in front of me now, looking into my eyes.

'Oh, it detonated,' I say. The whole terrible night flashes before my eyes. *Lu.* I have to clench my eyes shut for a second, overwhelmed by the guilt of having tricked Shell into letting me out of the dormitory, hiding in the bushes with Jake, breaking into Cranshaw's office and finding the device, then Florrie appearing, trying to disable it on the run, and Cranshaw and Florrie catching up to us. I swallow. 'We were on the school grounds, and my head teacher—'

'Not that one,' Rex says impatiently. 'The one *you've* got.'

I'm completely blank for a minute, thinking he must have got mixed up somewhere. Then I remember, and I feel the weight of the heaviest dread sink down from my shoulders and into my stomach.

'Oh,' I say, while Rex and the unit look at me expectantly. 'Yeah.'

'Well? Have you disabled it? Did Humans First remove it?'

I look down at my stomach. I don't even know if the device is in there, if that's where they would put it.

'Er . . . no,' I say. 'They didn't . . . remove it.'

'So it's still in there?' Rex presses. 'You can detonate it yourself?'

I clutch my stomach, taking a step back instinctively. Could the device go off at any time? Am I literally a ticking time bomb? 'I-I don't know—'

'Why didn't Humans First look after you anyway?' Rex leans back on the desk. 'Weren't they *proud* of you?'

I raise my chin up at his sneering face. 'I'm not involved with them,' I say, with as much dignity as possible.

Rex snorts. 'Yes, you are, they created you,' he says.

35

'You can't not be involved with them.'

I fold my arms. 'Well, I can. Not. Be involved.'

'We heard about your . . . crash,' he says, with a little smirk.

'In the police van?' I say. 'How?'

'It was all over the news.' He suddenly produces a tablet from nowhere. 'Pretty silly to let yourself get caught.'

'They were in my parents' house,' I say. 'They jumped me.' I feel a little flicker of hurt, again, at my parents' betrayal.

'And then making a beeline for Piccadilly Circus? Thought you could blend in with the crowd, did you?' Rex half rolls his eyes, but I'm distracted by the image on the tablet in his hand. A news report is flashing across the screen. The first thing I notice is that it isn't the Company news channel, but another one I've never heard of, called *One Second Update*. The second thing, the more important thing, is me: it's the helicopter feed from earlier. The square, the crowd, the tiny purple-haired figure running about haphazardly like a trapped ant. I disappear down under the drain cover, just as the police cars pull up.

'So close,' I say to myself, as the officers rush out of the car to the drain cover.

'Not really.' Rex sniffs. 'See what happens?' All four of the tiny figures have paused, standing in a circle around the drain cover – even from a distance you can see they're arguing with each other. 'None of them would fit down there. And they don't have units on patrol to do it for them, not any more.'

'Oh,' I say. I still have that prickly feeling at the base of my neck, that I-came-so-close-to-getting-caught feeling.

'Why didn't you go to Humans First?' Rex says. 'The engineering company's headquarters is full of those militant types, and it's so near there—'

'The police would check there first,' the unit cuts in.

'No,' I say, turning to glare at it. 'That's not it. I didn't even know. I'm not anything to do with Humans First, and I don't want to be. I only got told the other week that they even *made* units—'

'Oh, come on,' says Rex. 'That doctor . . . what's his name? The engineer guy?'

'Dr Tavish,' I say. Out of the corner of my eye I see the unit flinch. Can I not even talk about humans without offending units now?

'Yeah, that's the one. He performed updates on you, didn't he? The whole story's been all over the news channels. Meeting with him so often, you must have known.'

'I'm sorry,' I say as icily as possible. 'It never occurred to me I was a-a . . .'

'Unit,' Rex says. 'You can say it.'

'Anyway,' I say, flustered, 'what about you? Did Humans First have to tell you, or did you just magically figure it all out by yourself?'

The smirk drops from Rex's face. 'My situation is very different from yours.'

'Really?' I say. 'I find that a bit hard to believe, considering we're both—'

'I wasn't created by Humans First,' he says.

'Oh?' I'm completely thrown. There's more than one organisation producing units in the exact image of human children? 'Who then?'

Rex shrugs with one shoulder. 'I don't know. Some scientist my parents hired.'

'Your parents?' I say. 'Wait, what do you mean? Your *parents*?'

The unit starts to say something, but Rex talks over him.

'DX-9,' he says, and at first I think it must be some sort of secret message, but then he follows up with a world-weary 'please', and I get it. DX-9 must be the unit's manufacture code. I thought it was just a thing humans used to tell the difference between them. I didn't realise units used them as names for each other.

Rex has turned away from me. He circles back round his desk. 'My parents had a son. He died aged thirteen. So they had me created and downloaded all his memories into my brain.' He reels this off so quickly and without emotion it's almost robotic.

'Oh,' I say, feeling my face prickle. I don't know what else to say.

'Then when the law was passed, they had to tell me the truth,' he finishes.

'Why?' I say, without meaning to. 'I mean . . . why didn't they just keep it a secret?'

His eyes flash at me. 'My father is very important,' he says sniffily. 'It would have been damaging for him if the authorities had had to track me down. They were trying to avoid a scandal.'

'And then they kicked you out?' I say.

'No!' he barks, whipping round, suddenly seeming human again. 'I ran away. I wanted to join the other units.'

'Oh,' I say again. He *chose* to leave? He chose to come here?

Rex folds his arms, as if daring me to question him. Thoughts rustle round my brain like cockroaches.

'So . . .' I say, tentatively. 'The face . . .'

'At first I had trouble believing it.' He shrugs again. 'You'll do the same.'

No, I won't, I think, my hands going to my face. 'Well, that's awful,' I say. 'I'm really sorry . . .'

The remaining skin on Rex's face flushes. 'Don't!' he says. 'You don't have to be *sorry*.' His lip curls, as though my sympathy is repellent to him.

'OK, sorry,' I say. 'I mean—'

'It's a good thing,' he half shouts, jaw jutting forward. 'I finally discovered what I really am.'

'Good then,' I say. 'If you're happy.'

'I am,' he says through gritted teeth. Abruptly he turns away, sitting in the chair at his desk with his back turned to me.

There's a beat of silence in which the unit and I look at each other, and then away. I'm just about to speak again but I don't know what I'm going to say, when Rex's voice breaks the silence.

'So what are you going to do now?'

'Er,' I say, not really sure what he's asking.

He swings round, businesslike. 'Are you going to Humans First's headquarters?'

'No,' I say, instantly. I start to say, 'I can't . . . stay here?' just as Rex cuts across me with, 'You can't stay here.'

'What?' I say. 'You brought me here. Well, you got . . .' I gesture at the unit, still not sure whether to refer to it by its company code or not. Would it be insulting if I did?

'That wasn't an invitation,' Rex says, with a half-laugh. 'We weren't offering you *sanctuary*.'

'Well, why bring me here at all then?' I say, exasperated.

Rex smirks, shrugging. 'We were all just so desperate to meet the famous killerbot on a rampage through London, I suppose.'

'Me?' I squeak. 'I'm *not*—'

'Yeah, you turned out to be a lot less impressive in real life,' he drawls. 'I mean, I thought you would at least know what the deal is with the *bomb* you're fitted with. You seem like you've barely even realised you're a unit.'

'I did only just find out!' I say, but Rex ignores me.

'So we can't let you stay,' he says, as if it's final.

My face has gone hot. 'But—'

'You being here will have the police sniffing around,' he says, 'and they're already watching us, accusing us of causing trouble. If we're harbouring a fugitive—'

'A unit fugitive,' DX-9 cuts in unexpectedly.

'Still a fugitive,' Rex says. 'It's messy and we don't need

40

it.' He surveys me levelly, waiting for a reaction.

I swallow. 'I can't go to Humans First.' Dr Tavish might have helped me escape the medical centre, but that doesn't mean they're all like him. What if they turn me in? Or worse, start experimenting on me?

Rex and the unit say nothing. I can feel my chin wobbling but I can't-can't-*can't* cry in front of them.

'Where I am going to go? I don't have anywhere else.'

'That's not really my problem,' Rex says.

'Can I just stay for a night?' I say.

One night will at least give me a chance to plan what to do next, out of the way of the police. I'm pinning all my hopes on this now. I can't get cast back into the hostile outside world. I'm too scared.

'No,' he says shortly.

I side-eye him, irritated. 'You won't take pity on me for one night? A thirteen-year-old girl, completely alone in the world?'

Rex snorts. 'You're no girl.'

I feel a flash of anger through my chest, with an aftertaste of shame. I splutter at him, 'Well, if that's the case – if you're thinking of it *that* way,' I gabble, 'you can't stop me staying here—'

'I think I can actually,' Rex says, stepping towards me.

'Oh yeah?'

'Yeah,' he says, and looks meaningfully over to DX-9. The unit is suddenly in front of me, an arm extended.

'Sorry,' it says quietly, and before I can think, it flicks its

41

fingers gently against my shoulder – and I'm knocked back so hard I fly into the shop door, crash through it and slide three metres across the tiles outside. It happens so quickly I can barely register why I'm lying on the floor blinking. I sit up, bewildered but uninjured, amazingly. It didn't even hurt; I just wasn't expecting the impact, I wasn't in the right mindset.

The units are rushing towards to me, and soon they're surrounding me on all sides. I stagger to my feet before they can touch me. Rex and DX-9 have followed me out of the shop.

I hold my hands up. 'Fine, fine,' I say. 'You've proved your point. I'll go.'

Rex says nothing, just looks at me expectantly. The other units watch, like it's a play.

'Yes, I'll go,' I say. I feel my stomach shrinking into a tiny ball at the thought. I'd pick a whole shopping centre of units over fending for myself in the outside world again. 'Out into a city where danger lurks around every corner, where the police are waiting to swoop at any given moment, where I can't even trust my own parents . . .'

'Did Humans First construct you with the world's tiniest violin built in, or was it installed on a later update?' Rex says.

'If you're happy . . .' I say, flagging, 'to let one of your own kind be captured by the police, the *human* police . . .'

Rex rolls his eyes.

'If you're happy to do that . . .' I say, 'to let a . . . a

42

unit . . . face the big, bad human world . . . on her *own* . . .'

'I am,' he says.

'I'm not,' DX-9 suddenly pipes up.

'What?' Rex turns to face it. I whip my head round too, narrowing my eyes. A minute ago it sent me flying across the room; now it wants me to stay?

'Me neither,' says a unit at the back, and then more of the crowd join in.

'Me neither!'

'Let her stay!'

'She's dangerous to have around,' Rex calls back at the group.

'So?' says DX-9. 'She's one of us.'

And suddenly the units are chanting, 'One of us! One of us!' The air is filled with the sound of their electronic voices, all talking at once.

I glare at them. This must be some kind of trick.

One of the smaller bots, about the size of a cat, zooms right up next to me, by my leg, squeaking, 'One of us! One of us!' at Rex. I inch away from it, quashing the urge to kick it away.

Rex is blinking very fast, as if he can't believe what the units are doing.

'But it's illogical,' he yells. 'She'll attract too much attention to us!'

'If she gets caught, that will be bad for units as well,' a cleanbot near the front says.

'How?'

43

'The humans will have captured the most dangerous unit,' DX-9 says. 'She's powerful.'

'I'm not dangerous or powerful!' I yell back, instinctively.

Rex is looking at me, eyes narrowed. 'That's right. The fleshbags do think she's dangerous.'

He looks me up and down critically. I fold my arms, knowing I shouldn't say anything right now. But it's hard.

'Fine, she can stay,' he says eventually, then turns on his heels and goes back into the shop.

I look around at the units' faces. They look back at me expectantly, as if they're waiting to be thanked.

'I . . .' I start to say. But I can't. I spin round and run in the opposite direction, after Rex.

Four

My first few days at the shopping centre, I hide away from the units, lurking on the upper floors. It's three storeys high, full of empty shops. The units congregate on the ground floor in their hundreds, gathering mainly around the shop with Rex's desk in. I've come to think of it as his office, although I eye-roll at myself every time I do. Whatever he said, he *does* seem to be in charge. He's the only unit with his own room, after all. And there's something about the way they've set up camp around him, and the way they hover. Expectant.

I try to avoid the units completely, even though the clinking, whirring sounds of hundreds of bots together carries all the way to the top floor. I may be grateful for a place to stay, but that doesn't mean I'm one of them. I inspect every single empty shop, in detail, despite the fact they're all the same: a bare white box. When I get excited about finding a discarded hanger, I realise I've probably had enough of trying to distract myself.

I desperately miss the Woodland River Centre. Everyone at Oaktree complained about it because it was, supposedly, not as good for shopping as the ones in London, where the adult Company executives got to go. In London, all the shopping centres supposedly had huge flagship the Look stores, entire outdoor virtual-reality complexes, and sushi available at the Sammy's restaurants. Well, now I'm *living* at a London shopping centre, and it's way more rubbish than the Woodland River Centre ever was.

I end up watching the units from the top of the broken escalator, where they can't see me. There are so many different types. I don't think I've ever seen this many units all together in the same place. At Oaktree, the units only came out when something needed cleaning. Or food was being served. Or around the grounds, but they'd all be spread out, each one working on their own task. Here they do nothing, and they never seem to sleep or go outside. When I first started watching them it was like they were a single, giant mass of metal, moving and clanking about as one, but after a while I started to recognise individual types, and before long they all seemed totally different to one another. There are the big, machine-type units that must have been used for manufacturing in factories – they don't even have faces and they can barely move, although they do have long extendable arms. They also seem to leak a lot of oil on to the floor; there are puddles of it around most of them.

There are also all the miniature units we didn't have at school. There are loads of them, all scampering around, chasing each other, pinballing off the walls and back again. They must have a certain level of intelligence that saw them defined as units by the Unit Rights Act and got them sacked, although they don't seem particularly bright. They're more like an excitable group of toddlers or kittens. Some I can tell are mini-groundbots, probably used to prune small lawns or topiary, and some are leaner-looking, more like cleanbots, so I guess they were for cleaning hard-to-reach spaces. I haven't seen any mini-foodbots though. I suppose full-size foodbots can make snacks and canapés too.

Looping round them, everywhere, is a type of unit I've never seen before. They're not even close to looking human. They're flat and rectangular, made of matte black metal, swishing around seamlessly. On their front they've got a screen, flashing up images from around the shopping centre. Screenbots. They're used to film and show movies and TV. Some of them are flashing through TV channels, switching from the news channels to sport to that all-unit soap.

When the screenbots stop moving, other units gather round them, sitting down to watch in a circle on the floor, like humans in a living room.

And from this far away, they almost could be human.

47

I have to blink and refocus my eyes. These are *units. Units.* They are made of metal. They have blank, expressionless faces. They don't even have hair or skin. But they're sitting down, legs crossed, some huddled together, some walking around, some standing, all interacting with each other. Talking, they're constantly talking, the noise rising up at me as a collective, nonsensical electronic babble. A sound never heard at Oaktree is deafening here.

Some of the units are even wearing clothes. Not full outfits, but I see a few T-shirts, a hat, in one case a paisley-print scarf tied rather rakishly around the neck. Why? Why on earth would a unit want to dress up?

They all seem to spend the majority of their time either charging their batteries in the corners or fixing each other up. Bits of machinery and nuts and bolts are scattered all over the floor. It seems to be a massive free-for-all, with units using bits of themselves to help others out: a spare wire, a drop of metal solder to patch up a gap, even eyeball casings and cosmetic attachments like ears or teeth.

Occasionally Rex walks through the crowd like a king greeting his subjects, talking to everyone, bending down to listen to the little appliances and sharing jokes with the giant industrial units. The metal underneath his scar glitters in the fluorescent lights. I've been looking and looking, but I can't see any other units that look like us. From far away some of them could pass for humans, but close-up, in a human society, they wouldn't stand a chance. But Rex and I could – we *did*. There must be more than five hundred units here; are Rex and I the only two like us?

At some point during my third week in the shopping centre, one of the bigger factory units, who's really just an enormous chunk of metal, breaks down near the bottom of the escalator. DX-9 and a cleanbot zoom over to help, opening up a panel on the unit's back. I duck behind the handrail near the top step, so they can't see me. A screenbot joins them, then a few of the little appliances gather round. I can't help but watch as they pull out wires at speed, reaching in to press buttons on an internal control panel, unscrewing bolts in seconds with their fingers. They seem to know what they're doing, but it makes me feel sick; I have to clap a hand over my mouth when they yank out the industrial unit's batteries. All those wires now in a pile on the floor, it makes me think of human intestines, the oil leaking out as visceral as blood.

A tiny screw rolls out along the floor and hits the lowest step of the escalator. None of the units seem to notice. DX-9 has screwed the panel back on and a foodbot is jabbing at the unit's restart button, but nothing's happening. Should I tell them? I mean, it probably doesn't even matter. There must be a much more complicated reason why the unit's not working. It can't be down to one little screw. It doesn't matter if I say anything or not.

But I can't seem to stop watching. Can units die? I know they can be deprogrammed, and if they don't get updated regularly they keep slowing down until they're basically useless and they have to keep their batteries charged or they shut down. But can they just break and never properly recover? I don't know. I lean over the top step of the escalator and call down as quietly as possible.

'Oi!' I say. No one takes any notice.

'Hey! DX-9!' I yell. But DX-9 just carries on jabbing buttons on the industrial unit.

Rolling my eyes at myself – why do I even care about some unit I don't know? – I walk clunkily down the escalator steps and pick up the screw.

'Look,' I say, holding it out to DX-9, and every single unit in the room turns to look at me. The metallic creak of their heads turning fills the room.

DX-9 silently comes over and takes the screw from me.

'Sit with us,' it says.

'No, no,' I say, backing away rapidly, wishing I hadn't said anything.

'We have clothes for you,' DX-9 says, gesturing to a nearby wardrobe. 'You can have anything you want.'

I'm still in the hospital gown I woke up wearing in the medical centre. I clutch it around me.

'No, thanks, I'm fine.' I don't want to get involved, I don't want to get too close to them. I shift away from DX-9 and realise the screenbot next to it is showing my face. A minute ago it was reflecting my face back at me; now it's switched to a different image but it's still my face. It's on *One Second Update*, a ticker tape scrolling along the bottom saying: *Millie Hendrick: Killerbot or Human?*

'Does that have sound?' I ask, walking up to it.

The units gather around me, but for once I'm too transfixed on the screen to freak out.

Suddenly sound blares out of the front of the screenbot. A woman's voice is speaking over the images, which switch from my face to the image of a man in a suit making a speech outside a building.

'. . . disputes the allegations that a killerbot was running rampage on its highest-ranking school's grounds . . .' the voice-over is saying. My ears start buzzing; I can't hear anything else, except the occasional words filtering through. Words like 'medical tests . . . no evidence . . . legal battle'. The building on the screen is a company headquarters, *my* Company headquarters, I realise, my heart thumping, and the man in the suit is the Company's Head of Legal. My mum used to play golf with him. He came to our house once over the holidays and asked for liquid green mudge in a glass with a straw because he was a little bit over his optimum weight.

I stare at the screen, my eyebrows somewhere in my hairline, as the audio switches to his statement.

'Though we aim to assist the police in their investigation, we absolutely refute the allegation widely spread in the media that a killerbot was on the loose at Oaktree Boarding School,' he says. 'There is absolutely no proof. The pupil accused was regularly subjected to medical tests and nothing was found to be amiss. As far as the Company is concerned, this girl is a perfectly normal, human child. We refuse to take the word of Humans First, a terrorist

51

organisation, that Millie Hendrick is . . . is –' he stops, wiping his forehead . . . 'represented a danger to other pupils. We hope to find the child as soon as possible and return her to the heart of the Company, where she belongs.'

And suddenly he's gone and a helmet-haired newsreader is on screen. 'Updates on the Millie Hendrick case as soon as we receive them,' she says. 'Now, construction on a new skyscraper, the Splinter, made major progress today as two of the world's biggest companies merge . . .'

There's a pressure behind my eyes. The Company believes I'm human? *A perfectly normal, human child*. They want me back? They don't think I did the terrible things Dr Tavish said I had?

I didn't think it was possible. I thought I was definitely a unit. I believed everything Dr Tavish told me. If there's even a chance . . . If it could have been a lie, all along . . . For the first time in weeks, a tiny chink of hope opens up in my mind.

The report cuts away from the newsreader in the studio. The TV is now showing a giant, pointy, half-constructed building, covered in scaffolding.

'What . . . ?' I say. 'What was *that*?'

I'm talking to myself, but one of the units answers me. 'It's been on all day,' it says.

I focus, to see a crowd of units around me, watching my face.

'There's been loads of other stuff too,' another says.

52

'You're constantly on it,' one of the little ones pipes up from the floor beside me. 'They run updates on you all the time!'

'Me?' I say, looking round at them, and they nod in unison, making that creaking sound again.

'Your parents were on earlier,' DX-9 says.

'Really?' I say, turning back to the screen. I sit on the floor, the units surrounding me. Just for a bit. Just until the next news item is on.

The days go by quickly when all you do is sit on the floor and watch TV. It's difficult to have a concept of the hours passing at all. There's no sunlight, just the overhead fluorescent lights on around the clock. I don't ever go outside. And I never feel tired

Until suddenly I do. It washes over me abruptly, for no obvious reason.

At first when it happens I find a quiet corner in one of the back shops, where none of the units hang around, and crash out for a few hours. But after a while I simply close my eyes where I am, sitting in the main entrance hall, units all around me. I don't need darkness or quiet, and I wake up feeling exactly the same as before. No grogginess. It's almost like I'm powering down and powering back up. I quickly squash that thought. It could be trauma, it could be living in a different place, it could be anything.

The units are strangely interested in all my human foibles. The wardrobe-bots are delighted to be able to produce clothes for me, knitting me jumpers and sewing together scraps of denim to make jeans. At first I didn't want to accept them, but then the sheer stupidity of sitting around in a grimy hospital gown with a group of units decked out in hats and feather boas started to get to me.

The foodbots have only one thing on their minds. 'Do you feel hungry?' they keep asking, especially in the first few days. I don't, but the more they ask, the more I start to think about how long it's been since I had food. Was it on my last full day at Oaktree, or the day before? I haven't really thought about eating since I was in that motorway service station, but suddenly I'm thinking about caramel, and gingerbread, and bacon and mashed potato and roast chicken. All my favourite mudge flavours are vibrantly renewed in my mind. Halfway through a daydream about the taste of chocolate – specifically Shell and I gorging on chocolate-mousse mudge one day when the machines broke and gave us as much as we wanted – one of the little appliances (who claims it used to work in someone's car, dispensing warm foam-topped drinks) pipes up, 'Do you ever get hungry?' And my stomach rumbles loudly.

Units, I'm fast discovering, have more expressions than I thought. The group clustering around me looks at me with what I can only describe as glee.

'Was that *you*?' DX-9 asks. I nod, my face turning red. I don't know why I feel so much more embarrassed than normal.

'That's the noise humans make when they want to eat,' a helpful foodbot tells the screenbot nearest me, who's flashing up question marks on its monitor.

'They're basically just bags of liquid inside, aren't they?' DX-9 says to me. I take a second before I respond. If I correct them by saying, 'Yes, *we* are,' would that be rude? Then I remember they think I'm *not* liquid inside. And the reason they're so fascinated is not because I'm human. They're fascinated because I've been designed to be human.

Something nudges my elbow. A vending machine has glided up behind me. As I turn, a packet of generic hot-chilli-flavour mudge – except they don't call it mudge, not out here – drops into its deposit box.

'For me?' I say. The vending machine doesn't have a face, just Spend 'n' Vend written across it in pink italics, but I feel as if it's smiling or nodding or generally being encouraging.

'Thanks,' I say, bursting open the packet and inhaling the spicy smell.

And that's how time passes. I watch TV and wait for my face to pop up. I eat all the snacks from the Spend 'n' Vend we were never allowed at school. The units ask me questions about humans. I pretend to ignore their incredulous-bordering-on-mildly-repulsed tone.

It's easy to get addicted to the twenty-four-hour news channels. It's even easier when stories about you are constantly on them. I watch the footage of me nearly getting caught at Piccadilly Circus about a hundred times. Apparently the *One Second Update* 'experts' think I went into an attack stance at one point, when I bent my knees slightly. Some killerbots do that before launching themselves at their prey and tearing it apart with their hands, *apparently*. The police were wearing special unit-proof vests, designed to protect their organs from a unit's 'crushing apparatus', or 'arm', as one newsreader clarifies. There is much speculation as to where I had disappeared to when I escaped down the drain, including that I had run to the nearby building strongly rumoured to be Humans First's headquarters (*not likely!*) or making my home down in the sewers, possibly training the sewer rats into some kind of rodent army (apparently not a joke).

'She may have been fitted with a homing device, which would have led her straight to the heart of the Humans First group's secret location in London,' says one shiny-faced expert.

Pfft, I think. How much are they paying these people? Then I remember the first place I ran to, supposedly on autopilot, was my parents' house. *Do* I have a homing device?

They run shots of Oaktree's grounds, Cranshaw's obituary, hundreds of exposés into the rise of Humans First and its grip of terror on the world, seemingly on perpetual rotation. There are numerous panel debates, all called things like 'Are *all* units as dangerous as infamous killerbot Millie Hendrick?' and 'Are *your* children safe from units?', in which one woman ends everything she says with, 'Companies need to *know* their children are safe,' while banging the table with her fist.

I see my parents a few times, but they're not exactly weeping into the camera and begging me to return home safely. They're on Company duty so, dry-eyed, they just reiterate the Company spokesman's statement: that there's no evidence I'm a killerbot, and that only once I've been tracked down and contained and it's been proved, can legal proceedings continue. It's all legalese, but I'm flooded with emotion every time I hear it. The Company believes I'm human. My parents believe I'm human. They want me to come home.

DX-9 is sitting next to me one day while I watch the Head of Legal give another speech about me.

'Is this the footage from the trial?' it says.

'Huh?' I say, salted-caramel mudge from the Spend 'n' Vend falling out of my mouth. 'What trial?'

'The Company is being sued,' it says.

'No, they're not,' I hit back, automatically loyal.

'They are. Why do you think they keep reading out statements? They're being sued.'

'They're being sued . . .' It takes me a second to join the dots. 'Because of me?'

On the screen, two older people are being interviewed. I vaguely recognise them in a Company context, but I can't quite put my finger on it.

'We just want justice for our daughter,' the man is

saying, while the woman sobs into a handkerchief. They both have dark shiny hair that reminds me of someone. And then I realise: they're Lu's parents.

A shiver descends all the way from the base of my neck to the bottom of my spine. I cannot bear to look at the hurt and anguish spelled out on their faces. I did that, I think immediately. I did that, I did that, I did that.

Then that little chink of doubt – or hope – opens up in me again. *No, I didn't.*

'Lu's parents are suing the Company?' I eventually choke out. 'But they're employees. They're part of the Company!'

DX-9 gives a little shrug.

'But why?'

I can't believe I never noticed units' expressions before I came here. DX-9 could not look more uncomfortable. 'They believe it's the fault of the Company that the safety of their daughter was . . . compromised.'

'What . . . ?' I say. 'By me?' I feel a crushing shame as the huge weight of what people say I did clunks for the millionth time painfully into my stomach. Tears prickle at the corners of my eyes.

'That's why they keep releasing statements that you're human,' DX-9 says. 'That's their defence.'

'Oh,' I say. 'But they must really believe it, on some level.'

'Well, no one can prove it either way, unless they catch you,' says DX-9.

'Right, right,' I say, focusing on the screen again.

A few days later, I'm watching a dramatic reconstruction of the whole of Humans First's plot, from the very beginning – I thought I might find it difficult to watch, but so far it's just been an actor in a grey wig playing Dr Tavish, picking up unit eyeballs in his lab and saying, 'Yes. This'll do. Mwahhahaha!' – when I realise Rex is standing next to me.

'Millie,' he says, businesslike, 'what can you tell me about your battery?'

'Huh?' I say, startled. 'How long have you been—'

'Your battery,' he says slowly, as if I'm three years old.

'Er . . . I don't know,' I say. 'I don't even know if I have one.'

Rex sighs for a very long time. 'Every unit has a battery. You've seen them all charging, haven't you?' He gestures to the units around us.

'Yes . . .'

He bends down to my level. 'Did the doctor who told you what you are say anything about charging?'

'Er . . . um . . .' I try to think, but it's difficult with Rex staring at me. I don't know what answer he's expecting.

'I don't think so. He never mentioned it. Sometimes I—'

'Fine, fine,' he says through gritted teeth, closing his eyes and rubbing his temples energetically.

'Maybe I'm solar powered?' I have an idea. 'Aren't units solar powered sometimes?'

'Well, only certain versions,' Rex says, looking doubtful. 'And you've been indoors for weeks. You would have used up all your reserves by now.'

'Weeks?' I say.

'Yes, haven't you realised?' he says. 'It's autumn.'

I hadn't noticed. I haven't been outside since I got here. 'Oh, OK,' I say. I can't seem to think about this battery thing very seriously, it's just too ridiculous. Me, battery powered?

'Maybe I recharge through sleep?' I say. 'I sometimes fall asleep and wake up, like I used to.'

Rex looks at me, nose wrinkled. 'What? No. That doesn't sound right. Units don't *sleep*.' He's so dismissive I scramble to change the subject.

'You don't charge, do you? What kind of battery do you have?' I say. 'Maybe they're the same.'

'I doubt it,' he says immediately. 'You have to remember I was built to last for my parents' entire lifetimes.'

'. . . As a thirteen-year-old boy,' I add under my breath.

'So,' Rex continues sternly, 'they built me with a state-of-the-art battery that constantly renews itself. It never runs out.'

'So you can just live forever?' I say.

'Unless someone shuts me down manually,' Rex shrugs, faux-modestly. 'Then yes, I suppose I can.'

'Well, maybe I have one of those too,' I say. 'I mean, I was designed after you. So maybe they're more common now.'

Rex is shaking his head. 'You have to remember, I was built by the people who loved me most in the world, who just wanted the pleasure of my company forever,' he says.

I roll my eyes as subtly as possible.

'Whereas you were created for a purpose, and a purpose that would take barely months to achieve at that. You will have been fitted with a high-power short-term battery. It would maintain all . . . this –' he makes a sweeping gesture towards my unamused face – 'expressions, moods, complicated speech patterns and what have you, but not designed to last forever. Now you've completed your mission – or not completed it in fact – as it stands it'll probably burn out on its own.'

'Did you seriously just shame me for *not* exploding and killing my brother?' I say. Then I catch up with what he said in the rest of the sentence. 'Wait! What do you mean?'

Rex shrugs.

'I've only got a short-term battery?' I hold my stomach, as if that's going to help.

'They couldn't risk you needing to charge up, could they?' he says. 'They couldn't risk that with me either, but . . .' He sighs again. 'We're very different, you and I.'

'But . . .' I gibber. 'But – but . . .'

'I could be wrong.' Rex inspects his fingernails, as if he's bored by my anguish.

'Well, no offence,' I say (I don't know why I bother to say that – he's never worried about hurting my feelings), 'but you must be.'

I can't be slowly shutting down. Just a while ago I was a thirteen-year-old girl, at the best boarding school in the country, with her whole life ahead of her. OK, so I thought

61

I was about to be killed by murderous units on the school grounds, but I was wrong. It can't be almost the end already. I don't *feel* as if I'm shutting down. No. I refuse to believe it.

'Why do you want to know anyway?' I snap at Rex. 'About my battery?' Even saying it feels stupid. Like saying, 'Why do you want to know about my stripy lemur tail?'

'Just interested,' he says.

'Why?'

'You hadn't charged. I was just wondering.'

'OK, but I *do* sleep,' I say, trying to remember the last time I actually did. Three days ago? Four? 'So like I said, maybe that's how I recharge. I'm very special, you know. Dr Tavish told me.'

Or maybe I'm human.

'That sounds more like something's wrong with you actually,' Rex says bluntly. 'That sounds like your battery's already staring to malfunction—'

'Just shut up!' I say over him. 'Since when were you the expert on units anyway?'

'Since I found out I was one,' he says.

'Well, good for you,' I say, turning away from him back to the screenbot before he can give me a lecture about being ignorant and not researching my heritage.

But Rex's words stay with me, niggling at me, poking me, elbowing me in the ribs and jumping up and down saying, *Think about me! Think about me!*

'Why don't we go outside?' I say one day, trying to

drown it out. 'Anyone? Who fancies a walk?'

The units around me barely look up.

'Outside?' a cleanbot says.

'Yes,' I say. 'There's no reason for us to stay inside all the time, is there?'

I'm met with a chorus of metallic shrugs.

'No,' says DX-9. 'But there's no reason to go outside either.'

A screenbot flashes up a message on its monitor. *There's nothing out there. Nothing to do, nothing to see.*

'Well, maybe it's not about that!' I say. 'Maybe I just want some fresh air.'

They all look at me. If units had eyebrows they would be raising them right now.

'*Fresh* air?' says the cleanbot.

'Is the air indoors not breathable for you?' the screenbot asks.

'It's *breathable*, it's just...' I say, '...getting a bit claustrophobic in here.'

They all look at me blankly again. Even more blankly than usual.

'Fear of small enclosed spaces?' DX-9 says, like it's just looked it up in a dictionary. 'Why?'

'I don't know why, I just...' I'm starting to get frustrated. 'It's not really a question of why! This is how I feel. You have to accept it! You're not allowed to question it!'

'But that's not logical,' says DX-9.

63

'That's not the point,' I shout.

'Old human habits,' the cleanbot mutters in DX-9's ear.

'Oh,' DX-9 says lengthily, suddenly seeming to understand. 'If going outside will help you feel normal, Millie—'

'Oh, stop patronising me,' I say.

'—I would be very glad to come with you.' It looks around at the others pointedly. But they're already backing away, shaking their heads.

'Forget it,' I snap, slumping back down on the floor. The news is playing the same shot of the Company's Head of Legal that I've seen a thousand times now. I'm *almost* on the brink of asking the screenbot to switch over, when the image changes.

'Who's that?' I say, as another man's face fills the screen. There are bags under his watery eyes and his cheeks are pulled taut, as if he hasn't smiled in a very long time.

He's reading his own statement, in a voice that sounds like the tide on a pebbled beach.

'The Chief of Police,' supplies DX-9.

'The net is closing in. We will find her,' the man is saying. Someone off screen asks a question and he cuts across them. 'We will find her,' he repeats, directly into the camera. To me.

'He's been handling your case,' DX-9 says. 'He's been on TV a few times.'

'Well,' I say, shaken, 'let's hope he's not very good.'

The camera is drawing back to reveal a line of granite-faced uniformed officers lined up behind him. It's such a long line the camera can't pan back enough to fit them all in.

'So many of them,' I say to myself, awed.

DX-9 shuffles up next to me.

'It used to be units,' it says.

'What did?' I say, still watching the screen.

'The security team that kept the peace in London,' it says.

'What, the London Metropolitan Security team?' I say. 'Aren't they units?' And then I remember, of course they're not. I've seen them. I was arrested by them. They're one hundred per cent human.

'Not any more,' DX-9 says. 'They're pretty pointless, now the redundants have all been employed.'

'Redundants? You mean the humans without companies?' I say. It still sounds bizarre, like saying 'humans without inner organs'.

'You know,' it says, 'the Big Four set up the London Metropolitan Security arm so the redundants wouldn't get out of hand. Start rioting, swarming the company buildings or whatever.'

'What?' I say. 'There can't have been enough of them to do stuff like that.'

DX-9 and the screenbot exchange a look.

'Yes, there were,' DX-9 finally says, wearily. 'There were thousands. Didn't they teach you anything at that school?'

'Ye-es,' I say. 'But they said everyone who lives in London is part of a company.' They didn't actually *say* that in as many words; they just never mentioned that there were humans without Companies. I didn't think it was possible for anyone to live outside the system and still *live*.

I mean, Humans First is a company too small to be part of the Big Four, and look at all of *them*. And that's still – technically – a company.

There's another loaded pause from the units.

'They showed us population figures!' I say. 'We had to learn them by heart!'

I remember sitting in geography lessons, sunshine coming through the window, copying down all those endless figures on to my tablet. I can't believe I thought it was so boring. I can't believe I used to wish to be somewhere else, watching TV for hours instead. I'm living my dream right now, and it's terrible.

'Well . . .' DX-9 says, 'maybe they didn't think the redundant humans counted. Anyway—'

'What? They just lied to us?' I don't even know why I'm surprised. They lied to us about the plan to blow the whole school and all the pupils sky high if our safety was ever used as blackmail against them. They lied to us about being able to leave whenever we wanted.

'Anyway,' DX-9 repeats, 'when the *act* passed' – I've noticed whenever a unit mentions the Unit Rights Act they do a little sneer or stress the word in some way to show they disapprove – 'the securitybots were sacked along with all the others. They hired humans to take over.'

'Really?' I say. 'So who's this guy then?' I gesture at

the police chief's face on the screen. 'Just a random *redundant* man?'

'Oh no,' DX-9 says, with a half-laugh. 'No, no, no, no.' He pauses, then adds, 'You wish.'

'What?' I say, sitting up straighter. My veins are growing cold.

He used to be in charge of the unit department at one of the major companies, the screenbot supplies.

'So he's an engineer?' I immediately think of Dr Tavish. Which makes my stomach turn over.

'No,' DX-9 says. 'He didn't make units, he commanded them. He disciplined them, he kept them in check.'

'OK . . .' I say slowly. 'And?' At least he didn't make them think they were human and send them to kill their brother.

'I just . . .' DX-9 looks down at its feet. 'I shouldn't tell you really.'

Well. Now my interest is piqued.

'DX-9!' I say. 'You have to tell me!'

'No, really,' it says. 'You don't want to know.'

'Did he torture them?' I say. 'Deprogramme them? Make them work all hours of the day and night for no pay?'

'We all did that last one anyway,' DX-9 says.

'Give me a hint.'

DX-9's eyes shift from side to side. 'It involves a soldering iron.'

'OK.' I hold my hands up. 'You know what, you're right. I don't want to know.'

* * *

I sleep that night, and for the first time since Oaktree I have dreams. It's all DX-9's fault.

I'm running through the eerily empty shopping centre, feet clattering on the tiles. The police chief's face is suddenly everywhere around me, gigantic, closing in.

'Millie, Millie, Millie,' the face is whispering as I force myself across the floor. There's a *chug-chug-chug* noise coming from somewhere. I think it's my breath, but then I realise: it's my battery dying.

I abruptly run out of energy, slumping on the floor, and the police chief swoops down on me from above –

Five

'Noooo!' I yell. And then I open my eyes.

'Millie.' DX-9 is calling me. 'Milliiieee!'

'What?' I snap.

'Your brother's on TV,' it says.

'Jake? Jake is on TV?' I hurry over to join it next to the screenbot. *One Second Update* is showing a boy sitting in an office. Company headquarters, I realise. Is it my dad's office? I'm not sure. Jake looks exactly the same, so much so that I immediately call out, 'Oh, he looks exactly the same!' and DX-9 has to shush me. The only difference is a flesh-coloured plaster stuck on his temple. And his skin seems a little . . . greyer than usual? Something about his face seems odd, as if it's sagged in on itself.

He's sitting opposite a shiny brunette interviewer, who I remember from a TV debate when she kept saying,

'We just don't know how dangerous she could be,' and then tried to convince everyone I might be able to blast fireballs from my eyes. Her own eyes are a startling neon violet and her teeth a startling neon white. When she looks into the camera and speaks it's as if her eyes and teeth are jumping towards you.

'And you never thought, "Could my sister be . . . not human?"' she's asking, as if people have thoughts like that all the time.

'I didn't suspect.' Jake's words are clipped.

'Didn't you ever—'

'That's just what they told me,' he talks over her. He isn't smiling. It's so weird to see Jake's face so drawn and unanimated. There's a whirring sound and he jolts, looking at something off screen, his eyes wide. His shoulders have tensed up, like he's about to leap out of his seat.

'I've noticed you seem . . . uncomfortable around my screenbot,' the interviewer says smoothly. 'But aren't you a supporter of unit rights? Weren't you targeted by Humans First because of your connection to AIR?'

'I'm not a part of that any more,' Jake blurts out, dragging his eyes back to the interviewer as if it's a huge effort. 'I didn't realise. I don't support unit rights any more. I'm not involved with any political campaign groups. I'm loyal to the Company.' The last bit he says in such an even, measured way I can tell he's been briefed on what to say.

But still, my heart is pounding in my ears. Jake . . .

doesn't like units any more? He doesn't want them . . .
us . . . no, *them* . . . to have rights?

'Since the news broke about Millie, there have
been conflicting reports,' the interviewer's saying. 'Your
Company has said it will continue to believe she's human
unless it can be proved otherwise. What do you think?
Could Millie be human?'

Jake's eyes are darting all over the place. I can't tell
what he's thinking. My heartbeat speeds up further, and
sweat prickles on the back of my neck. Everything – my
whole identity – depends on his answer.

'If . . . If that's what the Company is saying, it must be
possible,' he says. Then his voice hardens. 'But there'd need
to be proof. Concrete proof.'

He's scared. The idea of me returning to the Company
scares him. My own brother.

I'm already clutching my face when the next image
flashes up on the screen. Shell. Straight away, I burst
into tears.

DX-9, beside me, jumps. I do literally *burst* – one minute
I'm just sitting there, the next there's snot everywhere
and tears blinding me, running in trails down my face, and
a weird choking, yelping, sobbing sound is hacking out of
my throat.

DX-9 gives me a look of revulsion. 'What . . . ?' it says,
eyes following the tears rolling down my face.

'Oil leak,' a cleanbot says knowingly from behind us.
'Happens to the best of us.'

71

'That's not oil,' DX-9 says, horrified. 'That's water. And . . . something else . . .'

'Shut up!' I choke, trying to wipe my face. I have never wished harder to be surrounded by humans, who would either politely ignore me or pass me a tissue.

Instead I'm stuck with units, who are now gathering around me to stare slack-jawed at the snot dribbling out of my nose.

'Is she crying?' says one of the groundbots. 'Humans cry when they're sad.'

'Can you all just shut up so I can watch this?' I splutter, leaning around them to keep my eyes on the screenbot. My friend Shell is on the screen. She's sitting in a garden, which I assume is at Company headquarters, and her blonde hair is arranged carefully on her shoulders, though she hasn't got any iris drops in. That isn't like her. She's wearing olive green clothes. Is that the day's colour? I feel a pang when I realise I don't know. There've probably been fifty colours of the day since I left, and I'm never going to know what they were.

'Sad? But . . .' DX-9 keeps looking from my face, to the screen, then back to my face. 'It's just a news story. Why is that making her sad?'

The groundbot shrugs, like it's saying, *Humans be crazy*.

'Will you just let me watch?' I yell, louder than I mean to. DX-9 flinches. The other units look vaguely offended.

'I . . .' I drop the volume of my voice by about ten decibels. 'I just want to hear what she's saying, OK?' I sniff.

The units drift away, all except DX-9 and the Spend 'n' Vend, which trundles up to me and dispenses a packet of rhubarb-and-custard-flavoured mudge.

'Thank you,' I squeak, my nose still streaming.

Shell is in shock. I know she is. Like with Jake, her face is pinched together, as if she'll never smile again, and her mouth keeps twisting around itself. Every time she's asked a question, she shakes her head at herself before speaking.

'We didn't know . . .' she keeps repeating. 'She looked . . . I mean, *it* looked . . .' She trails off, looking utterly lost.

'I don't understand,' DX-9 says, out of nowhere. 'Why are you *sad*?'

'She was . . . is . . .' I say, my voice all clogged up as if I'm speaking underwater, '. . . my best friend.'

DX-9's mismatched eyes keep flicking back and forth between me and the screen. 'But . . . But—'

'What?' I snap.

'That's not even really her,' it says. 'It's just an image on a screen. She's not really *here*.' He adds the last bit like I might not have realised.

'It's not that,' I say, still hiccupping. *I just really miss her*, I want to say, but how can I explain that to a unit that doesn't even understand what tears are?

'Why would you cry though?' DX-9 will just not let this go.

'Because!' I say. 'It reminds me – it's hard for me to—'

'I don't mean why in general,' it says. 'I mean, why would *you* cry?'

73

'Huh?' I say. 'Why wouldn't I cry?'

'Yes. Why would you be manufactured to cry? What purpose would it serve?'

I sit in silence for a minute, watching Shell shake her head on the screen.

'All it's doing is draining your battery,' DX-9 adds. A heavy chunk of dread drops into my stomach.

'Well, I –' I start to say. 'I'm very special.'

Even I don't sound like I believe it. DX-9 looks over at me doubtfully.

I sniff again. 'Dr Tavish said.'

DX-9 flinches and looks away quickly.

'What?' I say. 'You don't believe me?'

'No, it's nothing,' it says, eyes on the screen.

'You know,' Rex says from behind us, 'we could just make you a replacement.'

'What?' I say, whipping round. 'Have you been standing there, listening, this entire time?'

'Yes, I'm just *that* obsessed with your inane conversations,' he says.

'How do you *appear* like that, as if out of nowhere? And where have you been all this time?' I narrow my eyes at him. 'Do you have an underground lair or something?'

He rolls his eyes, probably at my inanity, and then my brain scrolls back through what he just said.

'What are you talking about?' I say. 'Replacement what?'

'For your battery, dummy,' he says.

'How?' I say. I know the units help each other out, but that's all spare wires and outer casing. They're not constructing life-long energy sources for each other.

'First, we need to figure out what sort of battery you've got,' Rex says.

'I told you, I don't know,' I say. 'Dr Tavish didn't tell—'

'I know you don't know,' Rex snaps. 'I mean, I don't really blame him for not giving you a rundown of your manufacturing details. It's not like you exactly catch on quickly, is it?'

'Hey,' I say.

'*You* don't know,' Rex repeats, 'but there could be a way to find out.'

Rex sits on the chair in his office, his fingertips touching in a tent shape, eyes skimming over the group of assembled units. Me, DX-9, two groundbots I haven't met before, and a cleanbot who I've seen sweeping up the same square metre of floor tiles about once an hour since I arrived. The others all seem to know why they're here; everyone except me.

'So,' Rex says, looking at me over his fingers, 'the plan is to get into Dr Tavish's hard drive at his Humans First office.'

'Huh?' I say. 'How? *Why?* . . . And *how?*'

'No need to *babble*. It should be fairly straightforward,' he says. 'We've worked out a plan, and—'

'You . . . you've been planning this?' I say. Did I miss something? Why is Rex so bothered about my battery?

'What? Did you think we were just going to turn up at the Humans First headquarters and *then* figure out how to break in? Throw a rock through a window?' Rex leans back in his chair, while the units snigger at me behind their hands.

'Well, I . . . wait, break in?' I say. 'You're going to break in? You can't hack the computer remotely?'

Rex rolls his eyes so hard he nearly falls backwards off his chair. 'Of course not!' he says. 'If you were an anti-unit terrorist organisation, would *you* let all your classified information flitter freely about in the air, where any unit in the world can access it?'

The units are giggling again. I fold my arms.

'So, what?' I say. 'Your plan is to break into their probably heavily guarded headquarters, somehow magically find Dr Tavish's office, somehow magically find whatever classified information you're looking for on his hard drive—'

'That classified information being your manufacturing file,' he says. 'With your data on it, including the life cycle of your battery and how you actually work.'

'What?' I say. 'He'd have kept that? He wouldn't have deleted it to prevent the police from finding it?'

'Yes,' Rex says. 'That information exists for every unit. They can't arrest him for *creating* you. You're the one that committed all the crimes.'

'But – but –' I bluster, thrown by the mention of my 'crimes'.

Rex takes advantage of my momentary silence. 'This is how easy it'll be. These two –' he points out the groundbots – 'hang around outside and access the Humans First network, overloading the system until it breaks, which will disable the security alarms. DX-9 enters the building from the sewers and tracks down Dr Tavish's computer. The groundbots turn the system back on so DX-9 can find your file and download the information on it to his own brain. Then they switch the alarms back off again so it can get out. *Bam* – in and out in thirty minutes.' He brushes his hands together in a *bish-bash-bosh* sort of gesture.

'Why groundbots?' I say.

Rex shrugs. 'Any unit could do it really, but groundbots are most likely to be hanging around outside a Central London building at night; they could be tending to the foliage.'

'And the . . . this one,' I say, gesturing at the cleanbot. I don't want to just call it 'the cleanbot', in case it's rude. 'What's . . . this one coming for?'

'Lookout,' says Rex. 'Even when the alarms are down, there still might be security guards around – *human* security guards obviously,' he adds, 'but still security guards. They might need distracting.'

'And what am I going to do?' I say.

'You?' Rex says, lip curling. '*You're* not needed. You're going to stay here and hope it all goes perfectly.'

'Huh?' I say. 'No, I am not. I have to go, surely.'

'You're way too recognisable,' Rex says. 'All the other units could be ones owned by Humans First, at first glance. If a security guard sees you, they're going to know you've broken in.'

'But you can't do all this for me,' I say. I feel touched at their concern, but it's too big a risk. 'You can't risk yourselves like this, just for my battery. We'll find another way. We'll get through this – together.'

There's a big pause while I look around at them and they look back at me. Just as I'm wondering if we should hold hands and sing or something, Rex stands up.

'We're going,' he says abruptly.

'Why? Why is this so important?' I say. Did I miss something? Why is Rex so bothered about my battery? He doesn't even seem to like me.

'It's not about you,' he says, as if he can hear my thoughts.

'Oh yes, me thinking a mission that could get everyone locked up in unit jail or, like, I don't know, experimented on by Humans First scientists –' the units, including Rex, all recoil as I say this – 'just to download a file about *me*, to find out about *my* battery and keep *me* alive, is all about me is just purely self-obsession.'

'Believe what you want to believe,' Rex says coolly. 'We're not dropping this on *your* say-so.'

'If it's about my battery, I should be allowed to go,' I say, an idea formulating in my mind. There's no way

I'm letting them go to Humans First without me.

'No,' says Rex.

'Yes,' I say.

'No,' says Rex. 'And that's final.'

'Yes,' I say. 'And *that's* final.'

'You want to leave here, go into central London and get caught by the police?' Rex says. 'You want to take that risk?'

'I won't get caught,' I say, possibly not as confidently as I would like.

'So one minute it's, "Oh, pwease Wex, pwease let me stay in your unit wefuge, otherwise the big bad humans will catch me and lock me up and it'll be all your fault,"' he says, pouting and putting on a squeaky voice.

'If that's supposed to be an impression of me—' I start.

'And now suddenly it's, "Why won't you let me go outside? It's not fair! I won't get caught! You're too mean!"' He stamps his foot, like a toddler having a tantrum. 'The police aren't even the ones you should be worried about. Do you know what Humans First will do to *you*, if they catch you breaking into what everyone knows is basically their headquarters? I mean, we know what they do to normal units, but *you*—'

'You said they'd protect me if I went to them,' I say.

'Yeah, but you didn't, did you?' he says. 'And if they catch you, they're going to know you're working against them, and the one thing they hate most is a unit with ideas above its station—'

'They won't do anything,' DX-9 cuts across him.

Rex raises his eyebrows at him. 'To *her*?'

'She's pretty much their mascot at this point,' DX-9 says. 'They'd stop her leaving, keep her safe from the police, taunt the Company with the fact that they've got her. She'd be treated better there than she is here.'

Rex's face twists in a way that means he knows DX-9 is right. And makes me wonder why I didn't go to Humans First for help. Oh yeah – they're evil.

'How do you know so much about Humans First?' I say to DX-9.

'I've dealt with them before,' he says, looking into the distance. 'I know that building inside out, top to bottom.'

I'm about to ask it more when Rex speaks. 'If you go, you'll be a spare part,' he says. 'There's no room in the plan for you. You'll hold everyone up.'

'Oh, is that why you're not going?' I say, unable to resist. The fact he keeps saying *we* when he'll be safe sitting here is irritating me to the point of distraction.

'DX-9 has thirty minutes to track down Dr Tavish's computer while the alarm system is down,' Rex says, like I haven't spoken.

'I know where it is,' DX-9 says softly.

'He won't have time to faff around with your fake fleshbag problems,' Rex finishes.

'I'm going,' I half yell at him. 'I won't slow them down, I won't get caught, I won't destroy this whole mission because I'm hungry or sleepy or something. I am going and you *cannot* stop me.'

80

I know this isn't the point, but I keep picturing it: DX-9 and me looking through the files on the computer in a darkened office, trying to find the right one – trying, and trying, and not finding anything. No file on the manufacturing of unit Millie Hendrick.

I don't understand, DX-9 would say. *It should be here.*

I think I understand, I'd say, looking dreamily into the distance.

Would that be 'concrete proof'? Would that be enough to convince Jake and the Company and the whole world that I *am* human after all? I don't know, but I need to see it with my own eyes. And what if there *is* a file on an illegal unit placed at Oaktree, but it's not me? What if it's been someone else all along? It's not impossible. Is it?

Six

The night of the mission one of the wardrobes provides an outfit of dark clothes for me. As I'm pushing my hair up into a black woollen cap, DX-9 outlines the route.

'Dr Tavish's office is on the second floor, and we'll be entering from the basement . . .'

'You've really been there before?' I say. 'How long were you . . . there?'

'A while,' it says. I wait for it to elaborate, but it stays silent.

'You were trapped there?' I say. 'In their labs? Did they kidnap you?'

DX-9 doesn't look at me.

'Are you sure this is a good idea?' I ask, as gently as possible. 'I mean, won't it be difficult—'

Its head whips up, its grey eye and its green eye equally

steely. 'I'll be fine,' it says, its voice harder than I've ever heard it.

'But, you—' I start to say, but it carries on with the plan, talking normally again.

'Now, to get from the sewers to Humans First's basement, we need to climb up a pipe,' it says. 'It'll be a tight fit, but it's not for very long, so it should be fine.'

'Oh,' I say. 'They just conveniently have a pipe leading from the sewers to their building? That's lucky.'

'Well,' says DX-9, looking at me carefully, 'I'm not sure how much you know about old buildings, Millie . . .'

'Er . . .' I say, not sure what's coming. 'Not much?'

'When the building was first put up, hundreds of years ago, it was famous,' DX-9 says in a this-is-the-start-of-a-really-long-story sort of way. 'The people of the time called it the Gherkin.'

'Gherkin?' I say. 'What's a gherkin?'

'That information has unfortunately been lost in the mists of time,' says DX-9. 'But it's safe to say it meant something like "majestic" or "towering". Anyway, the point is, when it was built, electronic toilets weren't widely used. So the basement room we'll be entering into is actually . . . a disused loo.'

It takes me a second to cotton on. 'Wait . . . *What?*' I say, my voice reaching hysterical decibels. 'The . . . So the pipe . . .'

The units gathered around me nod.

'But that's *disgusting!*' I say. 'We can't – we can't – I mean, that's not hygienic, surely?'

DX-9 shrugs. 'They haven't been used in about fifty years,' it says. 'No one ever even goes to the basement any more.'

'But . . .' I keep clutching my hat, as if my hair has already got germs in it. 'But they were used at *some* point, right?' I look at the cleanbot next to me, who doesn't seem to speak. 'You can't be OK with this, can you?'

The cleanbot just shrugs, along with the others. Of course they don't care. They're units. But *I* care. I could be human, for all I know.

'Having second thoughts?' Rex suddenly appears, uncharacteristically happy. 'Fleshbag habits taking over?'

What else can I say? 'No, of course not,' I say. '*I* don't care. I was just making sure no one else was bothered. Checking everyone else was all right with the plan.'

'It'll be fine when we're there,' says DX-9.

But when we are there, standing in the sewers below the Humans First building, it is not fine. It is most definitely not fine.

'We're going to crawl up *that*?' I say. The pipe's entrance is about the same width as a dinner plate. I have no idea how my shoulders are going to fit in there.

'I did say it would be a squeeze,' DX-9 says.

'That's a bit more than a squeeze,' I say.

'It'll be fine,' it says again.

'Units don't get claustrophobic, do they?' I say.

DX-9 and the cleanbot share a quick look. 'In a minute

the groundbots will have overloaded the system, we'll go up and it'll be over before you know it,' DX-9 says reassuringly to me.

The groundbots split off from us a while ago. Because they're shutting down the network there's no way to communicate with each other, so everything has to be done with exact timings. We have ten minutes to get to the super-computer, ten minutes to access it with the system turned back on, then ten minutes to get out.

DX-9 unscrews the lid from the pipe, and some old, brown water spurts out.

'Urgh, urgh, urgh,' I say, wishing anyone else here felt the same way as I do.

'It's just a bit of water,' DX-9 says. 'It can't get inside your casing or anything.'

'But . . . it's gross,' I say.

DX-9 and the cleanbot share another quick look and then DX-9 is climbing inside the pipe, clambering up. It disappears quicker than I expected. I look at the cleanbot.

'You first?' I say hopefully.

The cleanbot silently shakes its head.

'Are you sure?' I say, slightly desperately. 'I don't really want to get stuck between the two of you.'

The cleanbot just shakes its head again.

'OK, then,' I say, and put my head inside the pipe. At least there's no smell. I wriggle up, using my elbows and knees to pull myself forward. It's actually not as bad as I expected. As long as I don't think about rats. Oh God.

What if there are rats?

I reach the top, popping my head out and looking around. It's only then that I realise I'm looking out of a toilet bowl. My head is in a toilet.

'Urgh!' I say, scrabbling out and on to the bathroom floor, writhing about. I brush at my clothes while DX-9 watches.

'You're fine,' it says. 'It hasn't been used in—'

'It's the thought of it,' I say. 'You wouldn't understand!'

With the cleanbot out, DX-9 opens the bathroom door a crack and checks for security guards. When it waves us forward, we shuffle as silently as possible out into a long corridor, keeping low as we run for the fire exit at the end. The building is deadly silent and completely dark – which means the groundbots have shut the system down. We clank – well, the other two clank and I just step – up the fire exit's concrete steps until we reach the second floor. As I'm quietly feeling relieved that we're not heading for an office on the fortieth floor, DX-9 looks through the glass panel on the door to check the corridor's clear. I notice a chip-scanner on the wall next to it.

'Wait,' I whisper. 'Don't we need to . . .' I gesture at the device.

'System's down,' DX-9 says. 'It'll open by itself.' If it was Rex, I know he'd be making a quip about me being an idiot right now, but DX-9 is too polite.

'Oh,' I say. And it turns out, it's right. I didn't know the security systems were all so interconnected. We hurry down the corridor, DX-9 counting the identical doors, until we reach the fifth one on the left.

'This is the one,' he says.

'OK,' I say, not one hundred per cent sure what happens now. I mean, I know the cleanbot is staying outside to keep a lookout and DX-9 is going in to Dr Tavish's computer, but what is my role here? Hold the door open? Help DX-9 type? Apprehension is creeping into my stomach all of a sudden. Do I *want* to see Dr Tavish's office? What if I find out something I would rather not know? But DX-9 waves me forward, so I force down my thoughts and slip inside the room after him.

This is not a normal room. This is a lab.

A giant, dirty machine, churning, clanking, cogs turning and pistons whirring, belching oil out on to the stone floor, showering sparks overhead, sits in front of me. Another one, an arm's-length away, is stamping long sheets of metal into squares, which zoom on a conveyor belt into another hulking machine. The other side of me, a tiny needle delicately traces liquid metal in a spiderweb pattern, over and over again, forming the bones of a hand. It finishes one, which whirrs off into the distance, and starts another.

The floor is littered with metal cogs and screws, pools of black oil and sharp scraps of metal. The air smells of petrol and there are big yellow signs saying 'HAZARDOUS MATERIALS' hanging off every machine. A rack of unit heads is directly across from us, all with obvious expressions of pain on their forever-frozen faces. One of them has had the casing around its eye removed and wires are exploding out of it. Beyond the conveyor belt there's a low table with a unit's torso dumped on it. Its feet and hands, or someone's feet and hands, are spread out next it, with what looks like its elbow and knee joints too, but the rest of it is missing. I can see limbs and eyeballs and body parts everywhere – all made of metal.

These are not repairs like the ones that happen in the shopping centre every day. This is not lending a friend a spare wire you don't need. This is butchery. These units have been eviscerated, pulled apart. This is like finding yourself inside the lair of a particularly brutal serial killer.

My vision wobbles as my stomach turns over. I clap my hand over my mouth, dropping to my knees.

'Oh,' is all I can say for a minute or two.

'This is the wrong room,' DX-9 is saying. 'This is not an office.'

'What?' I gasp. I really think I'm going to be sick. 'Why did you come in here then?'

'I must have counted wrong,' it says, matter-of-factly. 'It must be the next one.' It pulls me up to my feet and hustles me out of the lab. After all my worrying about it having some sort of nervous breakdown, DX-9's fine and I'm the one struggling.

In the corridor, I tap DX-9. 'Why were the machines running? I thought no one was here?' But it's already pushing me through the door of the next room along.

This room is different. It's wide and open-plan, laid out

with a thick carpet and long windows showcasing the glittering London skyline. There are desks lined up in perfect rows, each with a dark blue screen floating gently above it, glowing in the darkness. Panelled doors lead off the main room, each with metal plaques describing 'services to engineering' decorating the walls alongside them.

'*This* is an office,' I whisper through the darkness at DX-9.

'Yes,' it says. 'Yes, it is.' I'm expecting it to confidently step forward to one of the doors, but it stays still.

'Well?' I say. 'Which one is Dr Tavish's?'

There's a long pause.

'I think,' DX-9 says ponderously, 'they may have changed things around a bit since I was last here.'

'What?' I hiss.

'Well, it used to be that one –' it gestures at the nearest door, which has a 'PRIVATE BATHROOM' sign on it – 'but obviously it's not any more.'

'For crying out loud!' I say, as loudly as possible while also whispering. 'You're supposed to know! That's the basis of the whole plan!'

'I know,' DX-9 says. 'But it's almost definitely one of these ones.' It makes a sweeping motion to include all twenty doors leading off the main office.

'It could be any one of them!' I hiss.

'Just be patient, Millie,' it says gently.

'Patient?' I snap. 'We're already running around a building we're not supposed to be in, in the middle of the night, and any second now the alarm system is going to come back on—'

'Shhhh!' DX-9 snaps at me suddenly, and I'm about to tell *it* to shhhh when we both hear the sound of a toilet flushing from the bathroom.

We stand there in absolute shock, staring at each other with wide eyes for a quarter of a second. I wonder if crawling through the toilet pipe has made me go insane and I'm now doomed to hear toilets flushing wherever I go, but then the door behind us opens, and a man walks out. A man I recognise.

DX-9 has ducked behind the bathroom door, but I'm totally exposed, standing in the middle of the room with nowhere to hide, frozen like a rabbit in the headlights as I look up at Dr Tavish. And he looks back at me.

If I thought my stomach turned over before, it's nothing compared to now; it lurches so violently up my throat I nearly collapse on the spot. The medical centre at Oaktree, the room where he told me I was a unit, seems to suddenly enclose me, as though neither of us ever left. My heart is battering at my ribcage.

For a few seconds nobody says anything. I can only stand there, deafened by my own pulse in my ears, quivering, as I watch Dr Tavish's face change colour from fleshy pink, to red, to a sickly green, behind his thick glasses. He puts his hands up, close to his chest, palms out towards me. Without realising it, I notice I've done the same thing. And I've automatically crouched slightly, defensively prepared if he makes a sudden movement.

'Millie,' he says at last. His voice squawks. He's scared. Of *me*. 'W-what are you doing here?' He's slowly backing away from me.

'I . . .' I say. 'Um . . .'

'How did you get into the building?' he shouts, suddenly loud in the quiet room, like a frightened dog barking.

I don't say anything. I stay very still.

'If you've come to hurt me . . .' he gabbles.

'What?' I squeak, my hands still up.

'I've called security,' he shouts, 'and they'll be here any second.'

'No, they won't,' I say. And I realise he's only a person. He's just a person. A human person. I make the tiniest of movements towards him.

'Don't come any closer!' he screams. 'I set you free. I stopped the police from catching you.'

'I need to know, Dr Tavish,' I say, slowly but unmistakably, advancing on him.

'What? What?' he says.

'You need to tell me . . .' I say, my hands rising towards his throat, 'is it the truth?'

Suddenly he falls forward, dropping like a dead weight against my shoulder. I sidestep out from under him and he slumps face down on the floor. DX-9 is standing behind him, holding one of the metal wall plaques high up in the air.

Seven

I can't do anything expect clutch at my face and repeat
'Oh my God. Oh my God. Oh my God . . .' for what feels
like minutes. DX-9 doesn't move either, just stands there
holding the plaque up, like a statue. Then I come back
into my head.

'What were you thinking?' I screech at DX-9. Dr Tavish
hasn't moved or rolled over or made any sound. I poke him
tentatively with my foot.

'Is he dead?' Is there a dark stain spreading on the
carpet around his head, or is the darkness playing tricks on
my eyes? DX-9 doesn't reply.

'What did you do that for?' I yell. 'I was just about to
find out . . .' I trail off. I don't know what I was just about
to find out.

'Did you know?' I say gently, thinking it's in shock.

'Were you just trying to stop him, or did you know that would –' I look down at Dr Tavish's body – 'hurt him?'

'Of course I did,' DX-9 suddenly snaps. DX-9 has never snapped at me before. Before I can say anything, a brain-quaking alarm blasts through the air so loud my organs all jump at once and I shove my fingers in my ears to stop them exploding.

'Our time is up!' DX-9 yells over the noise. Lights are flashing on and off and I can barely see it. 'The security system is back in operation!'

'What?' I shriek. 'Why's that gone off?'

'It must know the doors have been opened without a chip!' it shouts back at me. If I didn't know DX-9, I'd say it was panicking.

'What do we do?' I yell, hardly able to hear my own voice.

'In here.' DX-9 grabs my arm and pulls me into the private bathroom Dr Tavish came out of. In one movement it unscrews the toilet from the floor and lifts it up, but of course it's electric. There's no pipe leading down to the sewers, just a small square space built into the tiled floor.

'But there's no way out,' I shout. 'There's no way to escape!'

'It's enough for now,' it yells back, shoving me into the tiny space and elbowing in after me. I'm crouched right down, my knees up around my chin. DX-9 pulls the toilet back over us and screws it in place. We're squished right up against each other, my elbows pressing against

DX-9's cold metal side. The flesh on my arms has immediately gone all goose-pimply, even through my jumper. Apart from the alarm, muffled underneath the loo, the only sound is breathing – just mine obviously, as DX-9 doesn't need to breathe. It becomes so loud and laboured – *hrrrrgh-phooo, hrrrrgh-phooo, hrrrrgh-phooo* – that I feel a nudge in my ribs.

'Can you stop that?' DX-9 whispers to me.

Through the tiniest, hair's-breadth gap between the loo and the floor, we can see Dr Tavish's motionless body in the dark main office. The blaring alarm cuts out and two security guards rush in. All I can see is their shiny black shoes and the bottom of their brown trousers. They stop short when they see Dr Tavish, one of them taking a step back in shock.

'. . . One of the engineers . . .' I can hear someone saying. Voices are drifting in and out, words difficult to catch.

'. . . We've apprehended the unit responsible . . .' a voice says from outside the room. 'It was just standing outside . . . didn't even try to run . . .'

Even in the small space, DX-9 and I flinch. I can't turn my head far enough to look at its face, but I know it's as horrified as I am. *The cleanbot.*

'I don't know . . .' one of the guards in the room is saying. 'I don't even know the rules any more . . .'

'We're not allowed to deprogramme it,' another voice says.

'But it's just a machine,' the first one says. 'And it—'

A new voice, louder and deeper than the others, suddenly speaks up. 'No police,' it says. 'Just take the bot to the labs.'

DX-9's mouth drops open. My heart thumps so hard I have to put a hand over it, to stop it drumming its way out of my chest.

'What about . . . him?' the first voice is saying. There are three pairs of legs standing around Dr Tavish now.

'Anything could have happened – he could have fallen, he could have tripped,' the deepest voice says.

'*Tripped?* But—'

'We cannot have the police coming here and sticking their noses in. They're itching for an excuse to get inside . . .'

'But he –' the first voice stammers. 'I mean, shouldn't we at least take him to a medical centre first?'

'We can't have him found in the office,' the deep voice booms.

'What do you—'

'Look, wait a minute,' it says, then suddenly one pair of the trousered legs and the shiny shoes are walking towards us and right into the bathroom. DX-9 and I shrink down further into the tiny space. Then with a snap the light is turned off and the security guard leaves the bathroom.

'This is what we do,' he begins to say to the others, and the door swings shut behind him. I'm still shaking.

'What are *we* going to do?' I whisper at DX-9.

'Wait,' it says. 'Just wait.'

'Wait for what?' I say. 'We can't just hide here forever! There's no way out!'

95

There's nothing but silence from DX-9.

'We can't go back to the fire escape because the guards are out there,' I say, as if explaining to a child. 'I mean, you heard what they did to the cleanbot . . .'

DX-9 says nothing.

'What are they going to do to us?' I say. 'If they catch us —'

The full force of the danger I've put myself in hits me. I thought Humans First wouldn't hurt me, but that was because Dr Tavish had protected me. That awful day when he told me everything, he let me run away instead of handing me over to the police like he was supposed to. If he is dead, or at least unconscious, and I'm caught here, what will they do to me? What if Rex is right and DX-9 is wrong and they do hate units with ideas above their station? Will they break me apart, experiment on me like any other unit? Or, given that the security guards probably don't care that much about unique engineering feats, deliver me to the police for a reward? *We cannot have the police coming here and sticking their noses in*, the security guard had said, so would they really protect me? Or would they just hand me over as quickly as possible to get rid of me and avoid further scrutiny?

I grab DX-9's shin, the only part of it I can reach with my arm at this angle. 'What are we going to *do*?' I shriek in its ear.

'Wait,' it says again.

'Wait?' I yelp. 'That's all you can say? Wait? For how long? For forever?'

'The security system will be disabled again in thirty seconds,' it says.

I wasn't expecting that. 'What?' I say. 'I thought it had to come back on so we could break into the computer.'

'Yes,' DX-9 says, 'and twenty minutes later it was going to be disabled again. So we can escape. Our window to hack into the computer has gone.'

I open and close my mouth a few times, like a fish. 'I . . . But that means—'

'Here's what I propose,' DX-9 says, cool as anything, while I gibber like a monkey. 'We jump through the window.'

'Through?' I say.

'The ornamental gardens are directly below. Past them—'

'Ornamental gardens?' I say. 'Why would a terrorist organisation's headquarters need ornamental gardens?'

'I don't know,' DX-9 says, waving a hand. 'For entertaining guests on sunny days?'

'Guests?' I say.

'There's no time for these questions,' DX-9 says. 'We have to go—'

'But the guards are outside the door.'

'Oh, they've gone,' DX-9 says. 'They all walked away about five minutes ago. Didn't you hear their footsteps?'

'No,' I say. 'I didn't hear anything—'

'Too busy thinking of questions probably,' it says.

'DX-9,' I say, surprised, 'was that a joke?'

97

'Now! Go, go, go!' it suddenly yells in my ear, and we launch out from below the toilet, splintering the plastic and skidding over the bathroom tiles. DX-9 wrenches the bathroom door open and we run across the office to the window just as the office door opens, moonlight from the corridor window falling directly across us like a spotlight. We don't stop running, DX-9 is grabbing for my hand and we jump at the window, smashing through it, glass falling in shards around us, and for a split second I just hang in the cold outside air, the lights of London's skyline sparkling below me, and then I tumble down through the darkness and land neatly in a soft hedge. I look back up at the window and there are two security guards standing there watching us through the broken pane.

DX-9 scrabbles for my hand and we leg it across the soft wet lawn, hop over another hedge and reach the end of the garden. Between us and the street is a giant brick wall.

I baulk. 'You didn't say anything about this!' I squeak at DX-9.

'I would have if you hadn't asked so many questions!' it shoots back.

I look around to see if there's any other means of escape. Like a gate left helpfully open. But there isn't. 'What now?'

'This,' DX-9 says, and springs from the lawn to the top of the wall in one incredibly graceful movement. It even lands with its legs crossed.

I spread my arms. 'I can't do that!'

'Yes, you can!' it says. 'Just do it!'

But I can't. I *know* I can't.

A door opens in the building behind me, light flooding across the lawns.

'Come on!' DX-9 calls down.

'OK!' I yell back. I bend my knees, sticking my elbows out. There are voices behind me, people running. I just need to spring up, all casual, like DX-9 did. Just one big step. Right up there.

'Hurry up! They're coming!' DX-9 calls down

'Don't rush me!' I spring up, about two inches. 'OK, wait, just let me try that again—'

'Oh for –' DX-9 extends its arm right down towards me. I grab at it, nearly missing, and it pulls me up the wall. I scrabble at the top bricks, scraping my fingers, and haul myself over, just as the security guards reach the base of the wall below.

'You didn't need to do that,' I say, out of breath. 'I was about to do it.'

'I didn't think we had until next week to hang around,' DX-9 says, taking my hand and hopping down the wall on to the pavement below. We run down the street until we reach the nearest manhole cover. DX-9 twists it open and we shuffle down beneath it, back into the sewers.

On the way back to the shopping centre I can't stop playing those brief few moments with Dr Tavish back in my head. I keep my teeth gritted, hanging on to the back door of the subway train as DX-9 holds on, just like when it first brought me to the shopping centre. But I can't even look at it.

If only I hadn't been so freaked out when I first saw Dr Tavish. I should have started asking him questions right away. He looked exactly the same as when he was telling me I was a killerbot he'd constructed; same glasses, same hair, same white coat. If I'd been prepared, if only I'd had enough time to ask him if I am actually a unit or not.

But then the plaque came down, and it was over before I'd had time to think.

Maybe Dr Tavish wouldn't have told me anything. Maybe he would have said something to prove beyond doubt that I *am* a unit, that the memories of seeing the metal underneath my skin, and the way I acted when I first escaped, weren't just hallucinations or my mind playing tricks on me. They were real. All of it was real. But I'll never know now.

And on top of that, we didn't get into the computer. We didn't even come close. In fact, the whole mission was a massive waste of time because DX-9 had to hit Dr Tavish with that plaque. All we achieved was dooming that poor cleanbot to a lifetime of being trapped in a Humans First lab.

Why did DX-9 do it? It's not like Dr Tavish was attacking me. He couldn't call security because the system was still down. What did DX-9 think Dr Tavish was going to do? I mean, did it actually realise what being whacked over the head with a giant piece of metal can do to a human? I now glare at it, out of the corner of my eye, but it's not even looking at me. This is what happens when units get given too much freedom. They don't *care* about anything. They don't have the right amount of respect for human life, like we do.

I mean, like humans do. Oh, I don't know what I mean.

I sigh unintentionally, the slipstream of the train whipping my breath back down the tunnel. Will I ever find out for sure what I actually am? Unit or human? *Is* the Company just using tactics when they say there's no proof I'm a unit? I mean, I couldn't jump up that wall tonight. But what does that mean? Was I just not in the right mindset? Maybe I wasn't built to make those kinds of jumps. Maybe I'm not that type of unit.

I don't have any cuts or scrapes from jumping through a glass window, but that's not impossible, right? I mean, it's not unthinkable that I just didn't happen to hit any shards of glass at the wrong angle. That's not proof I'm a unit. It could have so easily been a fluke.

When I was trying to escape from Oaktree in the summer, I twisted my ankle running away from a group of angry units – at least I thought they were angry; I thought they were trying to kill me. But maybe they were just interested.

Anyway, I twisted my ankle. It hurt so much I could barely walk. Yes, I did still manage to get back to my dormitory, but surely I wouldn't feel pain if I was a unit? Why would they build me to be affected that badly by a twisted ankle?

When Dr Tavish first told me, I didn't believe him straight away. But then I remembered that when the device I was holding blew up on the school grounds, it had ripped the skin off my hand and I saw the metal skeleton underneath. And that seemed like proof. But I'd just suffered a majorly traumatic experience, not to mention nearly being blown to pieces. I could have easily been seeing things? And hasn't this whole experience taught me, if anything, that your own memories can't necessarily be trusted?

Those first few days on the run, I did things only a unit could do. But, at the same time, I wasn't thinking straight. I wasn't in my right mind. Could I have been confused enough that some sort of hysteria took over? When something *that* traumatic happens to you, don't you feel out of sorts for a while? Maybe I thought I was doing things that I actually wasn't. Maybe the van crashed for another reason. Maybe London isn't as far from Oaktree as I thought. Maybe that little motorway service station had its alarm system set off for another reason and I just *thought* it was down to me.

I don't do anything particularly unit-like *now*. I eat and sleep. I cry. I think differently to the other units in the centre. Even Rex.

Could Humans First have some sort of plot to pin this whole thing on me, something another unit did? Are they trying to trick me into taking the blame? And I just stupidly fell for it?

If I could get back to the Company . . . If they could see

102

I was me and not a bloodthirsty killerbot ... But I can't leave the safety of the shopping centre without risking being caught by the police. I got close enough to being caught tonight and I can't let that happen again. If only there was a way to let them know I'm where I am, then the Company could get me and protect me before the police swoop in.

An hour later I'm almost wishing I had been caught by the Humans First guards and shopped to the police. We're in Rex's office.

'So, you failed,' he barks at us.

'Well ...' DX-9 and I are sat in the chairs facing his desk, not looking at each other.

'You were inside the building, the security system had been switched off,' he says. 'It was all set up perfectly for you ...'

Weirdly, I'm fondly reminded of being told off in Welbeck's office at Oaktree. I can't believe I now feel nostalgic for being shouted at.

'All you had to do was find the right office ...' Rex is saying. DX-9 shifts uncomfortably in its seat.

'Well ...' I say. 'I mean ...'

They both whip round to look at me. I clear my throat.

'I don't want to drop DX-9 in it,' I say, 'but this whole mission – this whole disaster of a mission – I mean, really, it was all down to—'

'It was Millie's fault,' DX-9 cuts across me.

'What?' I squeak. DX-9 doesn't look at me.

'How can you say that?' I say. 'I didn't get us lost. I didn't whack Dr Tavish over the head with a—'

'If she'd just hidden when he came out,' DX-9 says over me.

'If you had known where we were going in the first place!'

DX-9 talks straight to Rex. 'She wasn't even meant to be there,' it says. 'She wasn't in the original plans; she didn't know what she was doing. She just slowed us down and got us caught—'

'You said –' I start. 'You were the one who said I should come—'

'That is true,' says Rex, also ignoring me. 'You weren't meant to be there.'

'It was to find out about *my* battery!' I say.

'So?' Rex makes a face.

'So, *I* should be the one finding out about this sort of thing.'

'And then she couldn't jump over the wall while we were trying to escape,' DX-9 adds.

I shake my head at him. 'You *grass*.'

'What?' Rex snorts, and then tries to look serious. 'You couldn't jump over a wall?'

'I-I don't know what happened!' I say. 'I just couldn't get any momentum – I was trying to spring, but—'

'I knew it was a liability, sending you,' Rex says, rolling his eyes.

'Hey!' I say.

'You do know why that happened?' he says. 'Why you couldn't jump over the wall?'

I pause. 'Yes,' I say slowly. 'Because I'm not really a—'

'Because your battery is failing,' he interrupts. 'That's the only explanation. Physical limitations don't apply to units. We're not like humans; we can do anything if we're programmed to. Unless we don't have enough battery power.'

For a second I feel a weird falling sensation in my stomach. The horror is almost too much to take in. Then my brain clicks into gear. That *can't* be the only explanation.

DX-9 coughs quietly. 'She was designed to be human – no human could have made that jump—'

'So?' Rex snaps. 'That doesn't mean she's not capable of doing it. She's made of titanium, for crying out loud. Look at how fast she ran here—'

'What about a much more obvious reason?' I say.

Rex looks up. 'What? That you're a substandard, badly manufactured unit?'

His insults shouldn't hurt me. But they do.

'Why are you so obsessed with my battery anyway?' I shout, standing up so quickly my chair falls backwards.

Rex swings his chair away from me. 'Oh, just go and watch TV or something,' he says. 'Go and eat food and live in denial.'

'*I'm* the one in denial?' I say, spreading my arms around at his ridiculous office. 'At least I haven't set myself up as

105

Chief Executive of Unit Central!'

Rex swings back round, his jaw jutting out. 'Go, or I'll kick you out this time,' he growls.

'Oh yeah?' I say, facing up to him. 'Try it.' I have a sneaking suspicion Rex isn't actually that tough. After all, he was built to hang around his parents' mansion for eternity. Maybe we're not all built for amazing feats. Maybe he and I are just, well, normal.

'Come on,' I say, bouncing on the balls of my feet. 'Fight me.'

Rex could not look less impressed. 'I want to talk to DX-9 alone,' he says.

'Are you scared?' I mock him.

He turns round in a flash and flings his tablet at me like a frisbee. I dip out of the way just in time and it crashes into a shelf.

'*Go!*' he yells.

'Fine!' I shout back, turning on my heel. 'If that's how you really feel.' I kick over one of the smaller shelf stacks in his office before storming through the glass doors, but neither he nor DX-9 reacts.

I march into the main entrance hall, heading straight for the Spend 'n' Vend. It seems happy to see me and doles out a packet of glycerine straws in fizzy pineapple flavour. At least there's one unit that seems to like me. The nearest screenbot is showing the unit soap all the foodbots love so much. A group of them are crowded around right now, transfixed. It's a repeat – they don't make new episodes

106

since all the showbots got sacked.

'Isn't there any news on?' I say stroppily, and the foodbots turn and glare at me like I've personally insulted them.

A second screenbot, showing *One Second Update*, sidles up to me. *Did you fight with Rex again?* ticker-tapes across its monitor.

I roll my eyes. 'Don't say it like that,' I say through the glycerine straws hanging out of my mouth. As much as the units seem to respect Rex, they also keep talking about the two of us affectionately as if we're two crazy fake-human kids, doing crazy fake-human things they don't understand. But I don't like being grouped together with him.

'He was being unreasonable,' I say loudly. 'And so was DX-9.'

I can't believe DX-9 tried to pin the whole disaster on me, especially after it ruined my *one* chance to talk to Dr Tavish. A cleanbot nearby starts giggling, setting off a little cluster of coffee machines and mini-fridges.

You kids, the screenbot says. If it had eyes to roll, it would.

'Stop it! We're not the same,' I say. 'That's offensive, you know. You can't just lump us all together.'

You are really, the screenbot says. *Both human-like, both abandoned by your parents*.

'My parents didn't abandon me,' I say. 'I ran away.' I judiciously edit out the part where they set up their house

107

as a police trap for me. 'And, hey, wait a minute, Rex wasn't abandoned either! He ran away too.'

At first, the screenbot says.

'What?' I say, a bit of fizzy straw sweet falling out of my mouth.

The giggly cleanbot near me taps me on the shoulder. 'Have you not heard this story?'

'What? What story?' I say.

'The one that Foodbot-507 tells,' it says.

'Which one's 507?' I say.

'Over there.' It points across the hall, then yells, 'Oi! 507!'

A foodbot decked out in a printed floral scarf and a bowler hat approaches us. 'Yes?' it says.

Millie wants to know about how Rex got here, the screenbot explains.

'Well . . .' Foodbot-507 begins, as if it's got this story down to a fine art. 'I used to work at Rex's parents' mansion, in the kitchens,' it says.

'Oh, really? What were they like?' I say.

The foodbot shrugs. 'Rich, I suppose. I don't know,' it says. 'They were humans. I rarely came face to face with them.'

I feel a little flicker of guilt in my stomach. I know if any of my parents' foodbots or the foodbots from Oaktree were here, I wouldn't recognise them. In fact, the only unit I ever knew that even had a name at Oaktree was Florrie. All the rest kind of merged into one big metal blur.

108

'Anyway,' the foodbot continues, 'Rex's parents spent all this money on a house on the moon.'

'Whoa,' I say. Only the richest of the rich have actual *homes* on the moon. I know the Company was working on its own base up there before I ran away, but no employees were living up there yet. And the people who live there need loads of visas and forms and checks before they can even start building.

'It was in the most upmarket precinct and it had all the luxury fittings: swimming pool, anti-gravity deck, tennis courts, topiary gardens, everything. They spent months building it, designing it, furnishing it. It cost them millions. But after it was finished, they never once visited it – at least never together, and not for longer than a day trip. Everyone had expected them to move up there permanently as soon as it was ready. But they didn't. It was just left empty for months and months. No one could understand why.'

The foodbot pauses, and then looks at me. 'I mean, no humans could understand why. *We* knew.'

'You did?' I say, confused.

'Yes. We all knew what Rex was, right from the start. I'm sure all the units in your life knew about you too.'

I suddenly remember all those little looks, those knowing glances from the units working at Oaktree. Sitting in the grounds and noticing a groundbot, watching me, from metres away. The foodbots trying to make eye contact when I was in the canteen. Florrie, in my world-culture exam, bending right down into my face.

'The thing was, humans have to be registered to go to the moon, even for a short visit,' the foodbot's saying. 'Rex's parents couldn't produce his birth records, because he didn't have any.'

'Didn't their son?' I say.

'His death had already been registered, although maybe they would have tried to smuggle Rex in if it hadn't.'

'But why would that be such a big deal? Units can go up there too,' I say.

'Yes, if they register as units,' the foodbot says. 'Rex's parents couldn't tell the authorities the truth without him finding out.'

'Right, right,' I say.

'Then when the act passed, of course they had to tell him,' it says.

'And he left, didn't he?' I say, shoving another glycerine straw into my mouth. 'He ran away.'

'He did,' the foodbot says. 'We were all sacked and had to leave anyway, and he came with us.'

I chew on my sweet, trying to imagine how Rex must have felt. Having a choice of whether to leave. Would that be harder than being forced away?

'He was angry,' the foodbot says. 'When we first left, he was so angry. He couldn't believe they'd lied to him his whole life. But his anger didn't last. We found this place and were setting up here. I mean, we didn't think we'd be here for long; we assumed we'd get moved on by the police. But we're units – we don't need much to make a place home. Except obviously Rex didn't know how to *be* a unit. After the first night he came out and told us he was going back home.'

I spit out my glycerine straw. 'What?'

'He said he knew he wasn't human, but he could pretend to be. It was better than this life.' The foodbot gestures at the shopping centre around us. 'Which we all actually thought was pretty great, compared to being deprogrammed or rusting out in the city with no shelter, but anyway . . .'

'Then what?' I say.

'He went back to his parents' house,' the foodbot says gravely, 'but it was empty. His parents had left for the moon without him.'

'Oh . . .' I say. For some reason I can picture it too easily: Rex walking through the front door, calling out for his parents, expecting them to be so happy and relieved that he's returned and being greeted by nothing. Emptiness. Silence. And it dawning on him that his only option is to go back and live with the units.

Then I realise the reason I can picture it so well is because the same thing happened to me.

'So that's why he's so angry at everything,' I say.

The foodbot laughs. 'Oh no, not at all. He was always like that.'

111

Eight

DX-9 and I don't talk to each other for days. I don't see Rex at all, but DX-9 occasionally walks past me, or sits near the screenbot I'm watching, and I have to fold my arms and stick my nose in the air until it moves somewhere else. The other units find this hysterical.

'What even is the problem?' one of the cleanbots asks me, gasping for breath. 'You don't want him to *sit* too close? In case . . . what?' Then it bursts into laughter again.

Then one day DX-9 does come up to me, holding a packet of cinnamon-spice-flavoured mudge. It knows how much I like it.

'I'm sorry,' it says, holding out the mudge.

'Sorry for what?' I say tartly.

'Sorry for blaming the whole mission on you when it was my fault,' it rattles off super-fast. 'Please accept

112

this ... food ... as a token of my deep regret.'

I fold my arms. 'All you did was get that out of the Spend 'n' Vend and walk over here.'

'Yeah, but it's the thought that counts,' it says, eyes twinkling. 'Isn't that what humans always say?'

Grudgingly, although not that grudgingly because it's delicious, I accept the packet of mudge and rip it open.

'Maybe we could go for a walk,' DX-9 says. 'Outside.'

I look up at it. 'Really? You actually want to?'

'Yeah,' it says.

I raise my eyebrow.

'OK,' it laughs. 'I don't *want* to. There's nothing out there. But I've never done it before, so I thought I might try it out ... ?' It holds its hand out to me, and after a moment, I take it.

And it turns out DX-9 is right. They're all right. There is nothing outside. Literally nothing. There's the shopping centre, a railway line, the grassy hillock I slid down. And then nothing. Just concrete stretching into the distance as far as I can see. Which isn't very far – we're surrounded on all sides by mist, which instead of being ephemeral and vague like mist is meant to be, is disturbingly-robust looking. And it's raining, enough that within minutes my produced-by-a-random-wardrobe-that-very-morning purple sweatshirt is soaked through.

The Spend 'n' Vend, which has followed us outside, seems to sense my mood and immediately doles out three packets of chocolate-chip-marshmallow mudge.

'Where are we going?' DX-9 says, watching me shiver pitifully. The water bounces off his finish.

'Um . . .' I say, not wanting to lose face. I don't want to turn this into another example of dumb things humans think are normal that the units will use to make themselves feel superior to me. Again. 'What about . . . over there?'

We walk over to the far side of the mall, me squelching, DX-9 clunking, the Spend 'n' Vend trundling. Here, if anything, there's less than nothing. Only mist.

Or is there? As we stand there, the wind blows and the rain eases off a tiny bit. And now I can make something out in the distance. The silhouette of a giant bowl or maybe a stadium. It's falling to pieces. Half of it is eaten up by rust. A weird squiggly red thing stands next to it. Some kind of building equipment that broke and rusted over the years? I can't tell.

'Where *are* we?' I say, half to myself.

'London,' DX-9 pipes up.

'I know,' I say. 'I just mean . . . this isn't like any part of London I've seen.'

'London is a very big place,' it says.

'I know,' I say. 'But compared to central London, it's like . . . where are all the people? Where are the skyscrapers?'

'This is far to the east,' DX-9 says. 'When the sea levels rose and flooded the south-east of England, the west side of the city became more and more developed as the east was abandoned. More and more companies left. After a while no one wanted to live here. Especially now all the

114

redundant humans have got jobs and can afford real homes.'

'What's with the mist? And the rain?' I say.

'The weather adjusters,' DX-9 says. 'The weather has to go somewhere. It comes here.'

'Oh,' I say, wiping rain off my face. 'So in central London . . .'

'They have sunny days all year round,' DX-9 says. 'The rain falls here.'

There's a beat of silence as we watch the rain fall in sheets over the rim of the stadium shell.

'How do you know so much?' I say. 'Weren't you trapped in Humans First's headquarters your whole life?'

It bridles, affronted. I fondly remember the days I thought units didn't have feelings to hurt. 'No. Not always. I once manicured the London grounds of one of the world's biggest companies.'

There's another little pause, awkward this time, while I try to think of something else to say that isn't about Humans First.

'And I had the whole network at my disposal,' it continues. 'I used to listen to Shakespeare plays while cutting the hedges.'

'Really?' I say. I feel slightly ashamed. I can remember all too well practically falling asleep in English literature classes at Oaktree, in no way acknowledging my privilege until I recall that, *now*, DX-9 sits around watching TV as much as I do. 'Why can't you access that stuff any more?'

'Haven't since I got made redundant by my company.' His little metal head is bowed. 'No network. No signal out here.'

'I thought it was just me, because I don't have a chip,' I say.

'Units don't need a chip,' DX-9 says.

'I know, I know,' I say, rolling my eyes. 'Units are amazing.'

There's another little beat of silence.

'So ...' I say, wondering if I can ask this question, 'Dr Tavish ... ?'

DX-9 jolts, straightening up, but doesn't look at me.

'You knew him,' I say. 'You hit him for a reason.'

DX-9 doesn't do anything that might mean its answer is yes. But it doesn't do anything that might mean no either. It doesn't do anything.

'I don't know if he was dead or not,' I say. 'He could still be alive. But the point is, you were trying to kill him. You wanted him dead, didn't you? You knew what hitting his head with that plaque could do.'

I don't know if DX-9 thinks I wanted Dr Tavish dead. Maybe he was trying to avenge me for some reason. Believing that, on some level, I wanted to kill him. Because part of me did. Part of me is glad, even though I don't know for sure that he's gone. Another part of me is even jealous I didn't get to do it myself.

But at the same time it doesn't help. Dr Tavish being dead, or possibly dead, does not make everything magically better. It doesn't solve anything, or give me any answers, or get me back to my old life.

I need to know why DX-9 did it.

'When you were . . . at Humans First,' I say, as blandly as possible, 'you met him, didn't you? You encountered him in some way?'

I'm staring at it so intently, that when it finally starts talking it makes me jump.

'I used to work in the gardens of one of London's biggest companies,' it says again, in a voice much quieter than before.

I almost say, 'You already told me that bit,' but it goes on before I can say anything.

'Then one day my rotator cuff came loose and they sent me to be repaired. I didn't know at the time, but only one hundred of me had ever been made. I had a limited-edition cachet. So one of the engineers stole me and brought me to Humans First's headquarters.'

There's a long silence, while we watch the rain slowly mist its way down.

'And they . . . ?' I don't know if I should be pushing it on this.

'They experimented on me,' DX-9 says. It bows its head again, water dripping off.

'That's-that's terrible,' I choke out. 'And . . . Dr Tavish was involved?'

'Didn't you notice my eye?' DX-9 says, looking up at me finally.

'The green one?' I say.

'He has a whole cabinet full of spare eyeballs that colour. It's sort of his trademark.'

It's right on the tip of my tongue, to say, *I don't have it.* But I know this is not the time.

And that doesn't mean anything anyway. If I am a unit, I've been created to look exactly like a specific human. He couldn't just stick a bright green eyeball in my face, when my eyes are meant to be light brown.

But that doesn't stop hope rising in me like a balloon.

'I escaped, eventually,' DX-9 is saying.

'How?'

DX-9 looks straight at me. 'The same way we got in,' it says.

'The same – oh,' I say. The toilets. 'Yuck.'

'I made it back to my old company and got my job back. And everything was back to normal, until the Unit Rights Act passed.'

'And you lost your job,' I say.

'I know the humans fighting for the laws thought it was a good thing,' it says. 'But no one asked us. No one considered what would happen if we weren't cost effective to our companies any more. And that's the thing with freedom – now they don't want to help us. They want us to stand on our own two feet without acknowledging that the reason *they've* got to where they are is because of *us*. But none of our achievements count for anything any more.'

We stand in silence for a moment. I wonder, if I ever do

118

make it back to the Company, if I could persuade them to employ DX-9. Or just bring it with me, somehow, and maybe the Spend 'n' Vend too.

'Maybe . . .' I start to say, but then trail off. I don't know if saying that would hurt DX-9's pride.

I don't know if my eyes are adjusting to my surroundings, but all of a sudden I can see something moving through the mist. Flashing lights, way up in the air.

'What's that?' I say, interested.

DX-9's expression doesn't change, but its voice is hard. 'Inside. Now.'

'What?' I say.

It pulls me across the concrete, back to the shopping centre, the Spend 'n' Vend wheeling madly behind us. DX-9 pushes the door open so hard it bounces against the wall with a bang.

'Police!' it shouts, its voice amplified, echoing through the hall like a gunshot.

Nine

Units freeze like antelopes who have caught the scent of a lion in the bushes, and then suddenly they're all running about, screenbots skidding, industrial units clanking and spilling oil, the appliances zipping all over the place.

My heart is in my throat as DX-9 yanks me across the floor.

'I need to leave. Let me go,' I shriek, trying to wriggle out of its clamp-like grip but it doesn't listen.

'We need to hide her,' a cleanbot at my side screams.

'No, I've got to get away,' I yelp, just as DX-9 says, 'What do you think I'm doing?'

'I can't hide!' I yell. 'I'll be a sitting duck!'

The sound of helicopter blades right outside stops everything. Literally, the whole shopping centre stops moving.

'They're here!' the small units start squeaking.

Footsteps tramp across the concrete outside. 'No!' I yell – I'm directly in front of the doors, glued to the spot. They'll see me the second they walk in. DX-9 pulls at my hand and we clatter – well, it clatters, I just stumble behind – across the shopping centre.

'Why – why have they come here?' I gasp, out of breath. 'Have they found out about – about Dr Tavish?' I should have known this would happen. He is dead, DX-9 killed him and now they're going to arrest me and I'll end up serving two back-to-back life sentences.

DX-9's eyes swivel to me. 'How could they?' it says, just as if we were quietly sitting chatting. 'Humans First would never tell.'

'They could have ways of finding out,' I wheeze. My feet are only moving on momentum now.

'They don't,' DX-9 says, then stops short outside Rex's office, so abruptly I slam straight into the glass door. It wobbles for an interminably long second while I try to steady it, but miraculously it doesn't break. DX-9 is already across the room by Rex's desk.

'She brought the police here?' Rex explodes as I run up to them. 'They tracked her down somehow? Followed her trail from Humans First's headquarters?'

'We don't know that,' DX-9 is saying, amazingly calm and measured considering the situation.

'Just hide me!' I say. 'Come on, we don't have much time.'

'Right, because I should go out of my way to help *you* out,' Rex sneers. 'After you helped ruin the mission.'

'The mission that was to find *my* battery information,' I snap back. 'The only one who's really going to suffer is—'

From behind us, the front doors of the shopping centre bang as they open. The clanking noise of the frenzied units abruptly stops.

'Everyone freeze!' a human voice yells.

All my digestive organs jolt as one. Before I can think, I throw myself across Rex's desk, banging right into him. I crash on to the floor and he falls backwards in his chair. The noise level is roughly the same as throwing a cymbal down the stairs.

We both freeze, me crouched behind the desk with my ankle painfully crushed underneath me, Rex halfway across the floor, legs still tangled up in his chair. Silently he narrows his eyes at me.

'What did you do that for?' he mouths.

I shake my head. 'I don't know!' I half whisper. 'Shut up!'

'You shut up,' he hisses.

'Both of you shut up,' DX-9 says in its normal voice, appearing suddenly behind the desk next to me.

'DX-9!' I put my hand over its mouth, but it doesn't help of course.

'They can't hear us from here, Millie,' it says, its voice sounding heart-stoppingly loud in the silence.

'You don't know that!' I hiss-whisper. 'Oh God, oh

God,' I say under my breath, putting my hands over my eyes. 'What am I going to do?'

'Go to prison,' Rex says, sitting up.

'Shut up, Rex,' I say.

'Yeah, they'll probably really like you in unit prison,' he whispers, knowing he's found a sore spot. 'You've got a lot of stuff the average unit doesn't have. You know, skin, hair. Fingernails.'

'Fingernails?' I squeak, automatically putting mine in my mouth.

'Don't *chew* them,' Rex says. 'You'll need them. They're like currency in unit prison.'

'What?' I say. 'You're just saying that.'

'No, it's true,' he says. 'You've got used to the units in here sitting around you, listening to your stomach rumble, wondering why you're crying, haven't you?' He curls his lip at me. 'Now just imagine how the units in prison will react. The killerbots – oh, sorry, I mean the *other* killerbots.'

'Shut up!' I hiss at him again.

'They won't sit around fascinated. They'll simply reach out and take what they don't have.' He reaches forward and ever-so-gently touches my hair. I squirm away from him, and he smiles. 'Fingernails first.'

'They won't take my fingernails. They can't,' I say, trying to keep my breathing even. 'It would hurt, it would really hurt—'

'Because killerbots really care about hurting their victims,' Rex says. 'They're constantly concerned that the fleshbags they're murdering aren't in too much pain.'

Outside, the sound of slow footsteps echoes around the entrance hall. They're spreading out, patrolling. I'm sure I can even hear the tiny click of a gun being cocked.

'Can't she just escape through the basement?' DX-9 says.

'Basement?' I say, taking my fingers out of my mouth.

The smile drops from Rex's face. 'No.'

'There's a basement?' I say. 'In this building?'

'There's a window down there,' DX-9 says. 'You could escape out the back way.'

'DX-9 . . .' Rex says dangerously.

'But how would I get down there without them seeing?' I say.

'There's a lift in this room,' it says.

'Lift?' I say. '*Lift?*'

'The basement is private,' Rex barks.

I whip back around, furious. 'Do you *want* me to get caught? Or do you just—'

'It's out of the question,' he says. 'Can't you go and hide upstairs?'

'What if they look up there? I'll have nowhere to run!' I squeak.

The footsteps outside are getting closer. In a matter of moments they'll be outside Rex's door.

'Please, Rex, please,' I say. I'm begging him. I grab his knee, the nearest part of him I can reach, and he snatches his leg away.

124

'There are things there you're not meant to see!' he says.

'I won't look!' I snap, resisting the urge to say, *I don't care about your stupid secrets, you stupid freaky unit child.*

He's wavering. I can see his eyes watching the glass doors behind me. He can hear how close the police officers are.

'Please, please, please,' I say. 'I won't look around the basement. I'll just focus on the window, and I'll be through it and gone.'

'Where will you go?' DX-9 says.

'I don't know!' I say. Why don't these units have any sense of urgency? 'Away!'

'You'll come back though, won't you?' it says.

'I-I don't know,' I say. Is it my imagination, or are DX-9's eyes wobbling? But I can't promise I'll come back.

The footsteps are at the door. They've paused. DX-9 and I abruptly stop talking.

'Oh, for goodness sake!' Rex hisses, then grabs me roughly by the shoulder. Keeping low, he pulls DX-9 and me towards the back wall of the room, crouching behind a shelf rack for a second, then scampers, crab-like, to the far-left corner. DX-9 and I scuttle behind.

Rex rips down a huge poster of a shiny, brand-new shopping centre against the background of a sunny blue sky and reveals a set of lift doors.

I gasp. 'This has been here this whole time?'

'No time to explain,' Rex says, jabbing at the button. The lift doors part with the loudest creak ever, only opening halfway, and the three of us squeeze in, sidling through the gap. Rex presses the emergency-exit button.

'Wait – are you sure that's the right one?' I say.

'It's the only one that works,' he says, through gritted teeth. The lift descends in fits and starts, jolting downwards with a sound like a hundred very bad violinists playing at once.

'You could have said it was so loud!' I say, my heart thumping hard in my throat. 'If they didn't know a lift was here, they certainly will now!'

'You were the one who wanted to escape,' Rex snaps.

'Can we focus for more than two minutes, please?' DX-9 says wearily. The doors open with a creak and Rex elbows his way out first, throwing a tarpaulin over a table directly in front of us and ripping printouts down from the wall.

'I don't care about your stuff, you psycho,' I hiss, as I squirm out of the lift and dart across the low, dark room to the beacon of the tiny window at the far end. I pull myself up on to the little sill. When I push the pane open I almost get blasted back by a gust of misty wet wind, banging my head smartly on the window frame.

'Ow!'

'Keep going,' DX-9 urges me, supporting my feet from below.

I stick my head and arms through the opening, scrabbling at the dirt outside. Immediately my fingernails are covered in mud, but it's not as if I'll need them for currency in unit prison now. Awkwardly I haul my left foot up, then my knee, then wriggle the rest of my way out and finally I'm fully outside, rolling around on the grass.

'Yes!' I say, leaping up. Then out of the corner of my eye I see a movement, far to the left of me. Behind the sludge-green bushes that surround me, at the very corner of the shopping centre building, a police officer is standing guard, holding a tiny device in the crook of his arm. A deprogrammer.

I slam down, back into the mud. Did he see me? Did he see me? Did he see me?

I feel my heart racing. If he's making his way over here right now . . .

Without thinking, I roll across the mud and slip back in through the window, crashing on to the basement floor. DX-9 and Rex jump about a mile.

'They're out there!' I yell breathlessly.

'So?' they both say in unison. DX-9 looks worried; Rex looks murderous with rage.

'You've got to go,' he barks.

'I can't!' I say, getting to my feet, trying to wipe the mud out of my eyes. 'There's nowhere *for* me to go.'

With an eardrum-blasting creak, the lift starts up again.

'What did you do that for?' I say.

'I didn't do anything,' Rex yells at me. 'It's coming back down!'

'What . . . ? What . . . ?' I can only stammer. The dial above the doors has lit up. The number '1' is illuminated, but as I watch it switches to 'B'.

'What now?' Rex shouts.

'I don't know. How am I supposed to know?' I scream back. 'I need to hide!'

'There isn't anywhere to hide!' he yells.

The lift stops. All I can see in front of me is Rex's face, frozen in the same expression of horror I know I'm wearing.

The lift doors open the whole way. But it's not a policeman; the Spend 'n' Vend is standing there.

'What do you think you're doing?' Rex immediately starts yelling. DX-9 and I collapse on each other in relief. The Spend 'n' Vend trundles out of the lift, making a wide circle around Rex, to reach me.

'Thank God it's just you,' I say, putting my hand on its glass front.

It immediately dispenses a packet of avocado-and-chilli-flavoured mudge, but I hold up my hand.

'I'm not actually that hungry right now,' I say.

'Oh no!' Rex is yelling again.

I look over at him. The lift is on its way back up, and as we watch, frozen, the sound of the doors creaking open and feet stepping in is clear.

Rex turns on the Spend 'n' Vend. '*You* led them to the lift!' he barks. 'This is your fault!'

I can't move. I'm stuck, utterly exposed, as the dial moves again, when the Spend 'n' Vend nudges me.

'No,' is all I can say. This is no time for food. Then I see what it's trying to tell me. Its frontage is swinging open.

'Me?' I say. 'In there?' The Spend 'n' Vend almost nods. At least, I'm sure it would, if it had a neck. Even though there's only a tiny space inside, in between the rows of snacks and drink bottles, and I'm not sure I'll fit, or that the door will close, or that they won't look there anyway and find me, the lift doors creak and I jump in. The front of the Spend 'n' Vend slams shut behind me.

For a second all I can hear is my own breathing, and the gentle fizz from a bottle of apricot-passionfruit juice drink right next to my ear. The door of the Spend 'n' Vend is solid, but through a tiny gap along the seam between the door and the machine I can see a strip of what's going on. This is just like Humans First's headquarters all over again. I watch, hugging my knees to my chest as two police officers step out of the lift doors.

Straight away I recognise the police chief. He looks exactly like he does on the news channels, although, if anything, he's even bigger. His watery eyes roam around the room, flicking over Rex and DX-9's faces without pausing, and he puts a hand on the shiny deprogrammer in his holster.

The other officer, a half-step behind him, jumps about a foot in the air when he sees Rex, then laughs at himself, rubbing his chest. 'I thought that was a kid for a second,' he says. He's younger and fatter than the chief. 'I was like, what's a kid doing in here? But then I saw that.' He strokes a finger down his own cheek. He's looking straight at

Rex but talking about him as if he's not here. 'Man, they look real though, don't they? I didn't think they could look that real.'

'Shut up!'

I'm surprised when I realise it's the police chief who shouted at him and not Rex, whose nostrils are flaring like he's about to breathe fire. The fatter officer takes a step back, as the police chief glares at him.

For a second, no one speaks. I want to close my eyes. I don't want to see the police chief slowly walking up to the Spend 'n' Vend, sealing my fate, but I can't not.

The chief takes a step forward and my heart stops, but he's moving towards the table. Rex makes an unconscious, jerking movement with his hand, but doesn't say anything. Why isn't he yelling at them, throwing them out of his secret room?

The other officer has gone over to Rex. 'You're a unit?' he says, quietly, looking down at him and squinting. 'Seriously? How did that happen?'

Rex – *Rex*, who never misses the opportunity for a good, extended I'll-show-you-who's-boss monologue – just frowns and looks away.

The chief runs a leather-gloved finger over the thick tarpaulin covering the table. For a second I think he's about to rip the whole thing off. What would it reveal? What would Rex do then? But he turns abruptly and now he's heading towards me. I press my hand over my mouth to stop myself screaming. Everything goes silent. He leans forward, almost nose to nose with me, looking right into the seam. I can see the tiny blood vessels in his eyes. I can see where his iris drops stop, the tiniest line of slightly greyer blue at the very edges. Who dyes their eyes the same colour they already are? I can see the folds of wrinkled skin, the lines running from his nose to his mouth. I hold my breath, afraid he'll hear it. He reaches his finger out, right into the seam, and brushes all the way down it, millimetres away from me. Then he straightens up, looking at his finger. He rubs the fingertip against his thumb.

And then he's turning. He moves away from the seam, out of my line of sight. He's going, he's going, he's moving on. But just as I'm about to let out the whole lungful of air I've been holding, he calls over to the other officer.

'Fancy a snack, Cooper?' he says. I flinch at the sound of his voice so close.

'What?' the other officer says, and the chief gestures impatiently at the Spend 'n' Vend.

'Do you fancy a snack?' he says slowly, as if talking to an idiot, and my heart turns to ice. Is he going to try to get something from the Spend 'n' Vend?

'It won't work without the right chip, will it?' says Cooper, and I close my eyes with relief. Thank God. He won't be able to take anything out.

'When you've got the sort of chip I have, things like that don't matter,' the chief says, waving his finger over the Spend 'n' Vend's monitor. It beeps. My whole insides turn to water.

'What do you feel like?' the chief says. He's enjoying this. He knows exactly what he's doing. If the machine doesn't work properly . . .

'Does it have that sour-cream-and-chive flavour?' Cooper says. 'The one they discontinued back at the station?'

'Well, let's see . . .' the chief says. His finger moves over the selection menu.

'Say it's unavailable,' I say under my breath, hoping the Spend 'n' Vend can hear me. 'Please.'

But I can almost feel the waves of apology coming from the machine around me. It can't; it's incapable of flashing up the 'unavailable' sign if the item requested is actually in stock. There's a *thunk* to my solar plexus as a block of mudge is dispensed into my back.

'Look at that,' the chief is saying, with obvious relish. 'Nothing coming out. I thought these machines usually worked instantly.'

'Well, it is old,' says Cooper, and the chief narrows his eyes, turning a half-centimetre towards him.

'We'll see, won't we?'

As his gaze moves away from the machine, I twist, bending my arm backwards in on itself, wriggling my hand between my back and the packets of mudge. My hip bangs painfully into the front of the machine and the chief's head whips back round. I pull the mudge out from behind me and chuck it into the Spend 'n' Vend's dispenser. It shoots out and hits the chief in the shin.

'Hey, it worked!' Cooper cries out, picking the mudge

132

up off the floor. 'Amazing, I love this stuff!'

The chief glares at the machine's frontage, his eyes ranging all over it. For a second he looks so incensed I think he's about to take the machine apart. But then, suddenly, he moves on.

I cannot let out the breath I'm holding without making a noise. I close my eyes, staying as still as possible, as quiet as possible.

'What have you found now?' Cooper says suddenly, his voice unexpectedly loud through a mouthful of sour-cream-and-chive mudge. My muscles jolt and my eyes flick open. I can't see what's happening from this angle. What has he found?

As if it can hear my thoughts, the Spend 'n' Vend gently rotates and now I can see the other side of the room. The chief is inspecting the window. As we all watch, he slowly picks up something tiny from the window frame and holds it up. It's a single blonde hair. *My* blonde hair.

Rex furiously turns, glaring directly at the Spend 'n' Vend. At me.

'So she was here,' Cooper says, as if it's his victory. 'She was here, but she escaped.'

The chief ignores him, meticulously taking a plastic bag out of his jacket and placing the hair inside it.

Cooper slowly shakes his head and takes another bite of mudge. 'So she got away from you,' he says, almost admiringly.

'You've said that,' the chief growls, quietly. Dangerously.

'Maybe one of the boys outside has caught her,' Cooper says excitedly, as they move back into the lift.

'Hmph,' the chief grunts, and just as the lift doors close he looks right at me again.

I don't get out of the Spend 'n' Vend until we're back upstairs and the police have definitely gone. The units gather in a crowd around the door as I climb out, my legs numb from being curled up for so long. The Spend 'n' Vend immediately dispenses a peach-and-papaya-juice-inspired sugar drink for me. I unscrew the cap but I don't really want it.

'It was just a raid. It's normal,' says DX-9. 'No need to panic.'

'I heard what he said, DX-9,' I say. 'They were looking for me. And they almost caught me.'

Nobody says anything.

'Didn't they?' I say, my voice cracking.

'Yes,' DX-9 says hurriedly. 'But it's not something to worry about!'

'How can I not worry?' I squeak.

Text is rolling across the monitor of the screenbot next to us. *They didn't really expect you to be here. They don't think you'd have come to find us, and they don't think we'd have let you stay. And now they think you've left anyway.*

'They still came here,' I say.

'More to keep an eye on us than anything,' DX-9 says.

'You know that's not true!' I shout.

'Yes, yes,' says a voice from behind us. Rex. 'It's all about *you*, Millie.'

134

'What?' I say.

'They used to do that before you even got here,' he says. 'Calm down.'

I try to think of something snappy to say back but I can't, so I just glare at him instead.

'I can't stay here,' I say, turning away. 'I have to leave. I have to keep moving.'

'Why?' Rex says. 'They didn't find you.'

I whip right back around. 'What? You want me to stay now? You were perfectly happy to let me get caught earlier!'

Rex half shrugs. 'I didn't *really* think you'd get caught.'

'You –' I say, exasperated. I try to line up my words in my head, so they don't get all angry and jumbled up when they come out of my mouth. 'Do. You. Want. Me. To. Be. Here. Or. Not?'

'I don't care either way,' he says quickly, but not entirely convincingly. 'It would just be stupid of you to go, that's all.'

'And what if the police turn up again?' I say.

'You'll hide again.' He shrugs. 'What's the big deal?'

'I'm putting everyone else in danger by being here,' I snap at him.

'Look, there's been one raid in five months. I don't think they're *that* interested in you.'

'Er, *hello*,' I say. 'I'm on TV all the time.'

Rex looks at the screenbot, which is showing a news story about the Splinter skyscraper nearly being finished.

'OK, not *all* the time,' I say.

'OK,' Rex says, drawing out the word. Then I hone in on what he's just said.

'Wait, did you say five months?' I say, whipping round. 'I've been here for *five* months?'

'Well, nearly six,' he says.

'What?' How has time passed me by? I've been sitting watching TV and eating sweets for nearly *half a year*? I'm supposed to be *on the run*. I can't stop in one place for that long. No wonder I've come so close to getting caught.

The Company, my friends, my parents, Jake – they've been waiting for me to come home for six months. And I've just been sitting around.

'That settles it,' I say. 'I have to leave.'

'Why?' Rex says, exasperated. 'Where are you going to go?'

'Home,' I say.

I dive into the crowd, looking for the wardrobe I used this morning. They don't all make clothes my size.

Rex chases after me. 'You can't—' he calls.

'Haven't you heard?' I say over my shoulder. 'They want me back.'

'What?' he says. 'Your *Company*?'

'Yeah, they believe I'm human,' I say casually, to annoy him. 'They want me to come back.'

'But you're not,' he says bluntly.

I pause. I don't look at him.

'Oh.' Rex laughs. 'Do you still think you might be? Really?'

'I—' I say, stung by his laughter. I'm not one of them. I'm not. Is it not obvious? 'Look, things don't really add up—'

'What?' he says. 'Someone *else* at your school was secretly a unit attacking pupils under cover of darkness?'

'No,' I say. 'You wouldn't understand.'

'You ran across the country to London, barely breaking a sweat. You don't sleep. You don't eat—'

'I do both of those things actually,' I say.

'You don't *need* to.' He rolls his eyes. 'You just do it out of habit.'

'That's not true!' I snap. 'I get hungry, I get tired – no one else here does!'

'Yeah, but they all have batteries that were built to last,' Rex drawls. 'Yours is probably already shutting down.'

I jolt with anger. I move as if I'm going to hit him, even though I've never hit anyone in my life! Not even Jake. But DX-9, appearing out of nowhere, holds me back.

Rex looks at me coolly.

'Look, it doesn't matter what your *opinion* is,' I yell.

'It does if it's also fact,' he says.

'The point . . .' I wrestle away from DX-9. '*The point is*, the Company believe in me, and if I can go to them without getting caught by the police, they'll protect me!'

Rex narrows his eyes. 'Why?'

'Why?' I say. '*Why* what?'

'Why would they protect you?' he says.

'Because they think I'm human,' I say, resisting the urge to add 'idiot'.

'No,' he says, like I'm the one being thick, 'I mean, what's in it for them? Didn't you basically undo a lifetime's worth of PR for them?'

A screenbot near us disloyally switches over to footage of the trial with Lu's parents. I scowl at it as Rex laughs.

'Oh . . . it's a *tactic*.' He's enjoying this a bit too much. 'They're not going to protect you when they find out you're definitely a unit. They'll shop you straight to the police.' He laughs in my face.

'No, they won't!' I shout. 'They love me! That's my family!' I gesture at the screen, where Lu's parents are crying again. I can't bear to look so I turn away.

'Oh, we *all* had families once,' Rex says languidly.

'I don't care what you say. I'm going.' I walk to the nearest wardrobe and jab at the buttons on its panel. *You can just ask, you know,* flashes on the monitor, but I ignore it.

'Don't,' Rex says from behind me, quietly. 'You can't.'

'Watch me,' I say, without bothering to look at him.

'No, seriously,' he says. 'I can't let you leave.' He puts his hand on my arm, heavily. I look at him. Are we equally matched in strength? I've never seen Rex demonstrate the strength that units have. Would I be stronger, if I pushed his hand away?

'Why?' I squeak at him.

Rex's face screws up, as if he's about to say something

138

difficult. 'We . . . need you.'

'You *what*?' My brain is going, It's a trick, he's lying, don't trust him.

'I think you need to see what's down in the basement,' he says.

Ten

He's made a model of the Splinter. It sits in the middle of the basement, on the table he covered with the tarpaulin. He's lit it with a single spotlight. DX-9 wipes a particle of dust off the smooth side. It looks to be a perfect replica, made of old scraps of metal beautifully moulded into the spindly triangle shape. God knows how he's done it. I put my finger out to poke the model, but Rex smacks my hand away.

'You're going to blow up the Splinter?' I say, shocked.

Rex slams his hand down on the table, making me jump.

'We're not going to *blow up* anything,' he says. 'This plan is completely non-violent. We're not like the fleshbags, you know. We're not bloodthirsty.'

'So,' I say, noticing the map around the model, marked

with the layout of the terrace and where all the drain covers are. 'You're just going to . . . what? Ask the humans nicely for everyone's job back?'

'This isn't relevant right now,' he says, pulling the tarpaulin back over the model. 'It's more of a plan B.'

'Why did you show me then?' I say.

Rex shrugs. 'So you're prepared when the time comes,' he says. 'What we really need to focus on right now is plan A.' He looks at me. 'And you need to pay attention.'

'All right. But I haven't definitely agreed to be involved or anything, yet,' I say quickly.

'Just pay attention!' Rex snaps. 'Now, DX-9.'

'Millie,' DX-9 says. They are both opposite me, sitting on chairs, leaning forward like I'm very slow. DX-9 even speaks in a new, teacherly-type voice.

'What have you noticed about all the units here?' it asks.

'She won't know,' Rex says immediately.

'What? Why not?' I say.

'You're just not that interested in units, are you?' Rex says.

'I am,' I say. 'I've been living with you all for months.'

'What is it then?' Rex says, leaning further forward. 'What's the weird thing about all the units living here?'

I try to think, scrolling through all the units in my head. But there are so many different types . . .

'No? Don't know?' Rex says.

'Yeah . . .' I say, playing for time. 'It's that . . . everyone's got . . . rechargeable batteries.'

'I told you,' Rex snorts to DX-9.

'Oh, fine,' I say, folding my arms. 'What is it then?'

'Housebots,' DX-9 says. 'Companionbots. Same thing really, I know they get annoyed when people don't distinguish though.'

'Housebots?' I say. 'But there aren't any house—'

'Exactly,' DX-9 says. 'No housebots live in the shopping centre. No companionbots. Why do you think that is?'

'I don't know! Is this some kind of test?' I say, throwing my hands up. 'Can't you just tell me?'

'The housebots didn't lose their jobs when we all did,' DX-9 says.

This stops me short. 'Oh,' I say, 'didn't they? Why not?'

'Think about it,' DX-9 says.

'Oh, stop it!' I say. 'Just tell me.'

'The humans didn't want to lose them,' Rex snaps. 'They agreed to give them pay, shelter, all the stuff that stupid act brought in.'

'But why?' I say. 'Why keep the housebots and the companionbots but no others? Even the foodbots and cleanbots that worked in people's houses are here.'

'Well, think about it,' DX-9 starts.

'DX-9, stop saying that!'

'No, I just mean . . .' DX-9 says. 'The companies replaced the units with redundants. But high-ranking company executives don't want other humans, especially non-company humans, in their homes, do they? And they

142

knew their companionbots; they'd *connected* with them. They were living side by side, speaking to each other every day . . .'

I think about Cranshaw and Florrie. There's no way, if things had turned out differently, that Cranshaw would have ditched Florrie and replaced her with a human.

'But that's not very fair,' I say. 'The new laws mean one type of unit gets better working conditions and you're stuck here.'

'*We're* stuck here,' Rex interjects.

'Whatever,' I say.

'But anger at the housebots is pointless,' Rex says, which makes me look up.

'All right then, if you say so,' I say. That's about the last thing I'd expect Rex to say.

'What we need to do is get them on our side,' he says, 'against our common enemy. If all the units stand together, then we have power. We can make our demands heard – we can get our jobs back, get a fair wage—'

'Common enemy?' I ask, before realising he obviously means humans.

'What we need to think about is what would make the housebots want to join with us,' he's saying. 'I mean, they have everything they want. Why should they care about the shoddy treatment of their unit brethren?'

He's actually waiting for me to answer. 'Er . . .' I say. To be honest, if I was a housebot, I wouldn't care if other units were being treated badly or not. I doubt I'd even realise.

143

'We have to *make* them care,' Rex is saying. 'We have to show them that *together* we are more powerful than the humans.'

'Right, right,' I say, even though Rex's plan is ridiculous. I wonder what kind of mudge the Spend 'n' Vend will produce when I go back upstairs. I hope it's peanut butter.

'Think about it,' he says. 'If all the units in the world were united, the fleshbags could do nothing to stop us. I mean, if we declared war against them . . .'

'War?' I say, jolted out of my mudge reverie.

'Not *actually*,' Rex sweeps the word away with his hand. 'Just hypothetically, if we declared war, the humans wouldn't even get to the starting line. They'd *have* to surrender immediately. Because they know a united unit force could wipe out humanity in days. Hours even.'

'OK . . .' I say, a bit more on edge now. I'm not sure if I like where this is going.

'Don't look so worried. We're not talking about wiping out humanity,' Rex says. 'Not right now anyway.'

'You know, you can just finish a thought and then stop talking,' I say.

'So if we show the housebots we're more powerful than the humans, if we show them we can offer them so much more than a wage and a roof over their heads, that we can achieve *everything* together' – I have a feeling Rex has been practising this speech – 'they'll resign en masse and the humans will be left powerless, with their civilisation in tatters.'

'And we can do all that peacefully?' I say.

'Of course,' he says. 'I mean, we don't let the fleshbags know that, of course. But we don't have to *do* anything. All we need to do is prove to the housebots that they'll be stronger if they stand with us than they are with the humans.'

'But how?' I say.

'They know we have the most dangerous unit in the world at our disposal.' Rex shrugs. 'It's only a matter of time. The housebots just need more proof.'

'The most dangerous unit in the world?' I splutter. 'Who's that? And how are you going to convince them to join us?'

Rex and DX-9 glance at each other.

'We thought we'd just ask,' DX-9 says.

There's a very long pause, while I look at them and they look at me.

'*Me?*' I squeak.

'Yes, you,' Rex huffs. 'God, for someone so technologically advanced, you are awfully gormless.'

'But *I'm* not the most dangerous unit in the world!' I say.

I might not even be a unit, I don't say.

'You're the one they fear the most,' Rex says. 'On the news they never even mention the fact that most of the world's units are now jobless, because they're too busy talking about how scared everyone is of *you*.' Something about the way he draws out the word 'you' makes me think Rex might be more jealous of me than he lets on.

145

'We've been communicating with the housebots,' says DX-9, 'and they are interested, they know how powerful you are . . .'

'But I can't do anything!'

'You don't have to,' says DX-9 soothingly. 'There's just a few things they're worried about, like your battery . . .'

I turn to Rex. 'Is that why you were so bothered about my battery lasting?'

Rex rolls his eyes. 'Does it matter?'

'Yes!' I say. 'What? Do you need to know my battery will last long enough to meet the housebots?'

'Partly,' says Rex, not looking at me.

'What do you mean, *partly*?' I start, but DX-9 cuts across me.

'The point is, Millie,' it says, 'they want to meet you.'

'I can't meet them!' I say. 'I can't persuade them to join with us against the humans. I don't even know if—'

'Don't say it!' Rex bellows.

'I'm not meeting them,' I say, folding my arms. 'I don't care. If they turn up, I'll run away.'

'They're not coming here,' DX-9 says. 'We're meeting them. At the head unit's house in central London. And they want you to be there.'

'Well,' I say, ready to rain all over their parade, 'that's just not going to . . .'

But I stop. If I run away now, on my own, I'll almost definitely get caught straight away and be locked up by the police. I'll never get back to the Company. I'll be stuck in unit prison with all the murderous killerbots. But if I agree to meet the housebots . . . If I go with the units, under their protection, to this house in London, well, then I could slip away. This place is in central London. It could be just streets from Company headquarters, where I need to get to, where I can claim refuge. I'm much more likely to make it back home *with* the units than without them. Maybe it's not such a bad idea after all.

'Tell me what the housebots want to know again?' I say.

We leave the next night.

Just like before, we all gather in Rex's office. Me, DX-9 and Rex are already there. We're just waiting for three foodbots, who volunteered to join us. Rex is sitting with his feet up on his desk.

'God, this must feel like déjà vu for you, Rex.' I can't help teasing him. 'Every day you're waving people off to go and do your dirty work.'

'Not this time,' he says. 'I'm coming along for this dirty work.'

'Oh,' I say, surprised. I look at DX-9. 'Really?' I say quietly. That could make it harder for me to get away.

DX-9 shrugs. 'He wants to . . .'

'Yeah, but what if he compromises the whole mission? It is *Rex*.' I'm clutching at straws here.

'By being the city's most wanted unit criminal, you mean?' Rex is eavesdropping. 'I think you've already got that one sewn up, Millie.'

'Ugh,' I say. 'I meant by being generally rubbish, but whatever. I'll go and get a hoodie from the wardrobe.'

'What? Because going incognito worked so well last time?' Rex snorts.

'I didn't get caught, did I?' I shoot back.

'Yeah, but they saw you,' Rex says. 'We can't risk that happening this time – if the humans find out the head housebot is in any way connected with a notorious killerbot—'

'Oh please,' I say.

'The point is, we can't let the humans get a sniff of what's going on,' Rex says. 'And as the housebots haven't even officially agreed to join us yet, I don't think they'd be best pleased—'

'Fine, fine, you've persuaded me,' I say. Anything to get him to shut up. 'What do you want me to wear? A disguise? A wig? Some kind of clown costume?'

'Maybe it's finally time to take the disguise off,' Rex says, his eyes glinting.

'Huh?' I say, confused.

'Maybe it's time to truly be yourself,' he says.

'I'm already myself,' I say.

'I'm talking about your face, Millie,' he says. 'It's time to reveal your true face to the world.' The metal under his scar glints as he rises from the desk.

I finally twig. 'You can't hurt my face,' I say, taking a step back.

'I'm not going to do anything,' he says. 'You're the one

that has to do it.' He smiles, walking towards me, and holds out his hand. A stubby little knife is clenched in his palm.

'What?' I say. 'I'm not going to cut open my own face—'

'It's not real pain, Millie,' says Rex, moving smoothly, closer and closer. 'It's just what you're programmed to think.'

'That's real enough for me,' I say. 'I won't do it.'

'Just take it,' he says.

'No,' I say, trying to squirm away, but he grabs my wrist.

'What are you doing?' I say. 'DX-9, stop him—'

'I'm helping you. You have to see!' He tries to push the knife into my hand, but I keep my fist closed.

'I'm not going to cut my own face!' I yell, as we grapple with each other. 'I don't want to – it won't be the same for me! I'll bleed!'

'No, you won't! It'll help you see the truth,' Rex puffs. 'Just take it!'

'No!' I yell, slapping the knife out of his hand. It clatters to the floor.

There's a beat of silence, while Rex and I look at each other with mutual hatred. I'm about to turn and leave right now, but I need to get to Company headquarters. And for that, I need to go with the plan.

'I told you – I'll wear a hood or something,' I say, breathlessly.

'You can't go into that house as a human. You have to

149

do this,' Rex yells, the ragged skin on his face fluttering. I can't help but think, No way am I going to get into Company headquarters with a face like that. Then I realise that's not even the issue. If I get cut like Rex has been, here, there's no medical centre or bandages or supplies. I'd bleed to death.

'Why not?' I say. 'This is ridiculous, Rex—'

'Humans recognise other humans,' he says. 'They'll recognise you like *this*.' He sneers at me. 'They won't see you as out of place if you're a unit. You'll just be another slave to them. They don't see units as individuals.'

'Yes, they do!' I shout. 'They can, I mean, *we* can – we can tell the difference.'

My brain reminds me that back at Oaktree I actually couldn't. All the units blurred into one back then. I could just about tell which ones were cleanbots and which ones were foodbots, but that was it, and mainly because they had totally different body types. I definitely wouldn't have been able to tell individual units apart from one another.

'This isn't like Humans First,' Rex yells, jumping to his feet. 'If the humans at this house find you, you *will* go to jail. For the last time, you are not human.'

'I'm not risking my face!' I shout.

'There is no risk!' Rex yells, darting towards me with the knife out again – I try to twist away, but he grabs my hair and pulls – the knife is scarily close to my face as I kick out towards his stomach – he doubles over, and the knife slips out of his hand falling towards me. I can't move from Rex's grip –

The blade just catches the edge of my jaw and I cry out in pain.

'Argh!' I say, clutching my face.

Rex steps away as DX-9 darts forward. 'I know it hurts, Millie, but it's not real.'

I take my hand away from my face. Bright red blood is staining my palm. I actually jump.

'What? That's blood!' I squeak. 'I'm bleeding!'

DX-9 looks at my palm, then my face, then my palm again, lost for words.

'Look at that! That's real human blood!' I say, waggling my palm in its face, my heart pumping harder. I am human. I am I am I am.

'What? That can't be right.' Rex is coming back over. I hold up my palm to him, as the three foodbots we've been waiting for walk through the door.

'Well, it could be. It's—' Rex splutters.

'It's what? What else could it be?' I say. I wipe my chin where the blood is congealing. 'You didn't bleed, did you?'

'Well,' Rex is still trying to explain, 'maybe Humans First did that, just in case—'

'You didn't bleed!' I say. 'I thought you were *the* most advanced unit.'

Rex rolls his eyes. 'You're obviously more advanced, of course you are,' he snaps. 'You were only built last year.'

I can't help laughing. I suddenly feel buoyant with

happiness. 'So one minute I'm so crap my battery's failing, the next minute I'm more advanced than you.'

Rex glowers at me as the foodbots gawp beside him.

'*Or* maybe I'm just human!' I finish triumphantly.

'You're not!' he shouts.

But I am. I don't even need Rex to agree with me. In a way I don't know if I even believed it until now, but now I do. My heart's beating so hard.

DX-9, crouched beside me, gently touches my jaw. A little shiver of pain flickers through me.

'Ow,' I say, flinching away from him. This is amazing.

'Is it real?' it says. 'Is it real human blood?'

'Of course it is! This is proof!' I say. I'm almost exploding with happiness. I can go to the Company with actual proof I'm human. Even the police will have to believe me. Everything's going to be all right.

'But – wouldn't Humans First build you to seem completely human?' DX-9 says. 'Wouldn't they build you with blood? And didn't you pass medical tests at school?'

DX-9 can't ruin this for me. I *know*.

'You can't just explain away every little thing,' I say. 'At some point you have to accept this as the truth!'

It looks at the drop of blood – my blood – on its fingertip. 'If only there was some way to test it.'

'None of you have blood, do you?' I say. 'Isn't that proof enough?'

Rex storms back up to me. 'You're still meeting with the housebots.'

I almost say, *What's the point?* But I still need to get to Company headquarters. I don't even know which way to go, and the police are still after me. I'll tag along with the units, then ditch them when we get to central London.

Eleven

As we're trudging through the sewers – me, Rex, DX-9 and the foodbots, who apparently just want to see the inside of a kitchen again – I remember what happened last time.

'Oh God,' I say, stopping short so DX-9 bumps into me. 'We're not going up through someone's old toilet pipe again, are we?'

Rex snorts. 'No, that's ridiculous. Who would even fit in one of those?'

DX-9 and I share a look. 'Er, us, last time, when we broke into Humans First's headquarters,' I say.

'What?' Rex spits, spinning round to look at DX-9. 'She's joking, right? You didn't really do that?'

DX-9 doesn't meet his eye. Rex has gone a bit green. 'I thought you were just saying that to freak *her* out!'

'Oh, now who's got the fake fleshbag problems?' I say.

DX-9 waits patiently until we've stopped sniping at each other. 'No, we're not going through the toilets. Not this time.'

One of the foodbots stretches an arm up to the roof of the sewer and unscrews an opening to reveal a dank tunnel with rungs leading upwards.

'That tunnel leads directly to Linden House's courtyard,' DX-9 says.

'Oh yeah, sure, let's avoid arriving in places via the toilets when *he's* here,' I say.

'Sorry, we don't all enjoy climbing through toilets, Millie,' Rex says smugly.

I ignore him and gesture to the tunnel's entrance, a good two metres above the hard concrete ground. 'How are we supposed to get up th—'

But before I can finish, DX-9 springs and grabs on to the lowest rung, hanging there for just a second before climbing out of sight. Rex looks at me quickly.

'You first,' I say to him.

'No, *you* first,' he shoots back.

The foodbots zip up the shaft, one after another, until it's just me and Rex, standing in the sewer. It occurs to me I've never really seen Rex do anything unit-like. Whatever he might say about unit abilities, I don't know if he can jump that far.

'Your turn, I think,' I prompt him.

'Oh no, don't let me stop you.' He holds his hands up in

a *ladies first* gesture. 'I'd *love* to see how humans do this sort of thing.'

My face twitches with hatred for him. 'Right then, I'll just . . .'

I flex my muscles, stretching my arms out and winding feet to loosen my ankles. Or something. I won't be able to do this. There's no way. I don't know what I'll do if I can't even get into the town house. I won't be able to reach the streets. I'll just have to go back to the shopping centre. I almost feel relieved.

'Any time. They're not waiting for us or anything,' Rex snaps.

He won't be so smug when he has to give me a leg-up.

'Right. Right,' I say, gearing myself up to attempt a jump and be laughed at by Rex. I look at the hole and bend my knees, just as DX-9 pops its head out of it.

'Sorry, Millie, forgot you might need a hand!' Its arm whizzes down and hooks me up, and before I can take a breath I'm level with the lowest rung.

'Oh,' I say, a bit bemused, as I scrabble to grab on to the rusty metal. 'Er, thanks.'

'You idiot,' Rex calls from below. 'I was waiting for her to make a fool of herself!'

DX-9 subtly catches my eye in the dark.

'Oh . . . sorry about that,' it calls back down after a second. It clambers up the pipe.

'See you up there then, I suppose,' I call down. Rex

doesn't respond. I wonder if I should hang around to see *him* make a fool of himself. But the tunnel is damp and cold and I want to get out of it as quickly as possible. I clamber up after DX-9. It's not as long a journey as the original one we took down to the sewers, and my head pops out of the hole almost before I realise I've reached the top.

We've emerged into a tiny dark courtyard with brick walls on every side. Directly in front of me, lit by a neon strip light, is a chunky metal service lift, in which DX-9, the three foodbots and a unit I've never met before are awkwardly crammed.

'In here, Millie,' DX-9 stage-whispers at me.

'OK, OK,' I say, pulling myself out of the tunnel and hurrying over to the lift. It's a squeeze. All the foodbots have ridiculously prominent elbows (perhaps it's better for whisking or stirring or something) and the other unit, who must be one of the housebots from the kitchens, doesn't seem to want to get too close to the rest of us. Florrie at Oaktree, the only house- or companionbot I've ever met, seemed like all the other units, apart from the fact that she was always a few centimetres away from Cranshaw. But this housebot looks totally different to the foodbots and DX-9, in a way that I can't put my finger on. It's taller and more streamlined. Is its face more like a human's? I'm not sure. I can't quite recall what a human face has that a unit face doesn't.

'Hello,' I say pointedly to the housebot.

Its eyes flick up at me, as if it didn't know I could speak.

'Hello,' it says back uncertainly, without meeting my eye.

'This lift leads straight up to the kitchens,' DX-9 tells me. The housebot nods once, without smiling.

'We're just waiting for Rex now,' says DX-9.

No one says anything. We're all watching the hole now.

'Should one of us go down and—' I start, but DX-9 cuts across me.

'He'll be up in a second,' it says.

Another long moment of silence passes.

'We do have to get back up there,' the housebot says.

'I know,' says DX-9.

The longer the courtyard remains Rex-less, the more thoughts begin to wriggle around my brain like magically replicating snakes. I really can't remember any situation in which Rex has acted like a real unit. I mean he *talks* a lot about being a unit and unit rights and how much he hates humans. But a lot of people *talk*. Cranshaw kept saying Oaktree was the only place we could be kept safe, and she turned out to be making it up as she went along.

Rex does have that wound on his face. That's how everyone knows he's a unit. There's no denying it. But maybe that's his only unit quality. I mean, why would his parents design him with super-strength or extendable arms or a limitless brain if they just wanted him to be their son for eternity?

Why would Humans First design *me* like that? If they

just needed me to blow up? Well, it's obvious: I was born, not designed.

'Do you think . . . ?' I say to DX-9, who's staring at the hole just as intently as I am. I don't know how to say this. 'I mean, that was quite a big jump up. You helped me—'

'He'll be here,' says DX-9, patting my arm.

The housebot huffs at us. 'We really are getting pressed for time now . . .'

But if Rex is a human in everything but construction, why does he get to be king of the units? Why do we all follow his orders all the time? Why is he the one leading this so-called revolution?

Why do you even care? says another voice in my mind.

Rex's head pops out of the hole. I can actually feel DX-9 relax beside me.

'Those stupid rungs,' Rex gasps, staggering across the courtyard like he's stumbled out of a war zone. 'They're impossible to hold on to. I kept slipping.'

He wedges himself into the remaining space in the lift, elbowing me in the ribs. 'Can you move over?' he snaps.

The housebot, whose mood doesn't seem to have lifted with Rex's sudden appearance, leans over and pulls the metal door across. We whizz upwards.

'We are very busy tonight,' the housebot starts. 'We're fulfilling an awful lot of . . . *other* duties –' its eyes flick quickly over to the foodbots – 'that we weren't designed to do, and we are very stretched—'

'That's the whole point,' Rex drawls. 'So the fleshbags

won't notice there are extra units right under their nose.'

The housebot flinches when Rex says 'fleshbags'. I knew I was right to find that offensive.

'Indeed,' it says, 'and it is very important they do not discover you. Especially as we haven't agreed to anything, and may not ever—'

'Yeah, whatever,' Rex says. 'I'm not here to talk to *you*. I'm here to talk to FL-17. Not an underling. The leader.'

The housebot hates Rex. I can tell. It doesn't say anything else and I try to catch its eye, like, *Yeah, I think he's a prat too.* But it's not looking at me.

We judder to a halt and it slides the door open again.

For a moment all I see is steam, and the nostril-prickling smell of burnt garlic hits me like a wall. My stomach grumbles. It may be *burnt* garlic, but I haven't smelt real food in such a long time. The steam begins to disperse as soon as I step out of the lift and I can see the whole kitchen, panelled with steel cupboards and a giant fridge, which is bursting with hastily shoved-in vegetables and cheeses. There's an overflowing bin, its slightly sour smell hanging in the air, and a huge double-fronted steel oven, which has about eight over-boiling pans, lids rattling, on top of it. The housebots are hurrying around, flustered, holding tea towels and wooden spoons awkwardly out in front. They don't really look like they know what they're doing: one's hovering over a sizzling pan of onions on the hob, its eyes scanning all over the place in quiet desperation; another's using an ancient-looking plastic blender to liquidise a whole avocado, complete with skin and stone. There are plates of canapés haphazardly stacked everywhere. Some red pepper and mozzarella bruschetta slices are tumbling slowly to the grimy tiled floor, landing one by one with a splat. Another housebot bursts through the kitchen's swing doors and examines the nearest plate of mini-quiches, holding it up almost to its nose.

'They're fine,' the onion-sautéing unit snaps from across the room. 'They're good to go.'

'Just checking,' says the other housebot. 'Humans can't digest broken glass. You do know that, don't you?' It sweeps out of the room, while the housebot by the hob looks murderous

'*One* broken measuring jug, near *one* plate of cheese puffs, *once*,' it hisses at the housebot using the blender. 'And now he brings it up every single time I make anything!'

The foodbot next to me is staring so hard at the blender with the avocado I can almost see the blaze from its eyes, like an invisible thread across the kitchen. It's so intense I honestly expect the blender to explode any minute.

The foodbot on the other side of Rex leans over to us. 'They don't even have *blending attachments*,' it says in the first one's ear. 'They have to use *appliances*.' The first one slowly shakes its head, mute with rage.

The housebot from the lift seems hesitant, but Rex isn't.

'Hello?' he barks into the kitchen. 'We're supposed to be having a meeting—'

161

'As I said, we're very busy,' the housebot says, almost under its breath.

Rex doesn't seem to hear. He moves further into the kitchen, like he lives there. 'Where's your leader? We're here to see FL-17. And *only* FL-17. We won't talk to just anyone.' He knocks a tray of canapés with his elbow and about fifty little salmon-and-cream-cheese pinwheels cascade to the floor. The housebots rush over, distraught. One attempts to dust the worst of the floor's grime off the pastry, but if anything that seems to make the foodbots more upset. They've gathered together, frozen, their hands up by their faces. Rex by accident or deliberately, I can't tell at this point, steps on a rogue pinwheel, squishing it, and one of the foodbots clutches its chest.

'It's a bit of a shambles in here, isn't it?' Rex says loudly, while DX-9 looks away, embarrassed. The housebots, on their knees on the floor, look up at him. How we're going to persuade them to stand with us against the humans, I don't know.

I mean, how Rex is going to persuade them to stand with *him*.

One of the foodbots picks up a pinwheel from by its foot and surreptitiously tastes an edge. 'You know, dill would go nicely with these,' it says quietly.

'You're not supposed to be eating that,' one of the housebots snaps.

The foodbots share a look. It's very obvious the housebots cannot handle running a kitchen. They are

162

constructed to do the most basic chores and make polite conversation. I wonder if they're doing all the household work now. I'd like to see the state of the grounds outside.

'Look, please just show us to where your leader is,' DX-9 says quietly to the housebot from the lift, 'and we'll be out of your hair.'

The swing doors open again as a housebot comes through. I catch a glimpse of the outside room, where the event is taking place. It's panelled with dark wood, a glittering chandelier hanging from the ceiling. I strain my neck, trying to get a look at the faces of the people, but all I can see is coiffured hair and shiny bald heads, with the occasional metal unit head moving through the crowd. There's a video banner playing across the room, showing a new building development or something. Boring.

The room is almost full though. I could so easily slip out and none of the housebots would be able to catch me without drawing attention to the fact they let a group of rebel units – one a wanted criminal – into their humans' house. I don't recognise the room, but something about the wood panelling looks familiar. Didn't Company headquarters have the same panelling in its rooms?

Rex grabs my arm, jolting me. 'Let me talk first,' he mutters in my ear. 'Alone. You wait outside. Got it?'

'What? When?'

'We're going to the leader's office now,' he says, pulling my arm. But the housebot leading us through has heard him.

'She's the one we want to see,' it says, pointing at me. 'You're just delivering her.'

'*Delivering* me?' I say, alarmed, but no one hears me because Rex is shouting over me.

'Hey, I'm the brains of this operation,' he says. 'She's the . . . brawn.'

'You can say that again,' the housebot mumbles under its breath as it turns round. The image of Rex breathlessly wrenching himself out of the tunnel in the courtyard surfaces in my mind and I mash my lips together to prevent myself laughing.

'What was that?' Rex says, dangerously. DX-9 puts a hand on his arm, and for possibly the first time ever, he doesn't make a big deal of it.

'Fine, whatever, we'll both go in together,' he says, glancing over at me as if I might be the one about to scupper this whole plan. As *if*.

The housebot knocks on a door in the corner of the kitchen, then opens it a crack. It sticks its head in, nods, before pulling the door wide and letting us through. I'm thinking how a few months ago I didn't even know units had or wanted their own offices, and now this is the second one I've been in. I don't realise who the unit sitting behind the desk is for a few seconds, until I feel its eyes on me. I look up.

It's Florrie.

Twelve

I reel backward. Rex's hand clenches on my upper arm, trying to restrain me, but I shake it off, elbowing him away, and make a dash back to the door.

'Stop!' he yells behind me. But I don't. I fumble for the handle, then shoulder the door open and fall forward into the kitchen. I crash into DX-9, who's standing just outside. Without hesitating, DX-9 pushes me right back into the office, where, carried by my momentum, I trip over my own feet and stumble to the floor. DX-9 has followed me in and, clearly feeling guilty, drops down to crouch next to me, a hand cupping my elbow. All this time, Florrie's gaze doesn't flicker; her blue eyes just follow our movements across the room.

The moment I can speak again, the words come out in a shriek: 'She tried to kill me!' It tumbles from my mouth like a stream of air bubbles underwater.

'You have to talk—' Rex begins, but I shout over him, loud enough that the bots in the kitchen will hear.

'She did! You weren't there,' I gabble, pointing at Florrie, although my hands are shaking. 'She tried to kill me, and my brother, and my friend L-L-L—'

'Did I, Millie?'

The voice is such a surprise I actually whip round to see where it's coming from. It sounds as cool and calm and electronic as a recorded announcement.

'Did I try to kill you?' Florrie says again.

Automatically I duck down behind DX-9, looking back at Florrie from over its shoulder. I never heard Florrie speak when we were at school. I never heard any units talk at school. I didn't even realise the Oaktree ones could talk.

Rex said we were meeting FL-17. Unless . . . I nearly smack my own head. It's Florrie's manufacturing name. Of course *Rex* would show off by not using her human-given name.

'Just answer the question,' he says in a bored voice.

'Did I try to kill you?' Florrie repeats. Her voice is blank, inflectionless. Though I'm pretty sure she wants to kill me right now.

'You . . .' But as I start to argue, realisation slowly sinks into my spine.

'No,' I say, very, very quietly.

'Did I kill Lu?' Florrie says, her bright blue eyes searing into my face.

My heart drops about a hundred million miles. It's like waking up from a nightmare and nearly collapsing in relief when you realise it was only a dream, but in reverse.

I try to swallow the lump in my throat. 'No.'

There's another little pause, a tiny stretch in time, and I know she's about to ask me who did kill Lu.

And if she does, I don't know what I'm going to say. It wasn't me.

How could it have been me? That horrible tumbling feeling in my stomach, like I'm falling in a broken lift, is happening again.

Florrie's still glaring at me. The sulky, defensive part of my brain is stirring. Of course it wasn't me. I'm human. I fold my arms and avoid her eye.

Everyone in the room seems to have frozen. Even Rex isn't making sniping comments, for once. Then Florrie speaks again.

'Now,' she says slowly, 'can we talk, one on one? Unit to unit?'

I automatically bristle at the word 'unit'.

'Wait a minute,' I say, my voice sounding half swallowed, tiny and weak. I clear my throat and look Florrie dead in the eye. 'You *did* try to kill my brother.'

It's not like I could easily forget that night. Jake and I had stolen the device from Cranshaw's office, the device she was using to hold the Company to ransom. We were trying to enter the codes to disable it when the door slammed shut behind us. Florrie had caught us. We escaped across the grounds, still trying to enter the codes, when something slammed into Jake so hard he was knocked to the floor. Florrie. Her eyes on mine, she crushed Jake into the grass, her forearm across his neck. I can still hear the choking, gurgling sound he kept making.

I shudder inwardly at the memory.

Florrie sighs heavily. 'What would you have done?' she snaps.

'Huh?' I say, momentarily wrong-footed.

'Two children. As far as Cranshaw knew at the time, two children had stolen the device that, if fully detonated, would destroy *everything*. Plants, buildings, machines, humans. Everything within a three-mile radius,' Florrie says. 'What would you have done? Let them play with it and patiently wait for it to be returned?'

'That's not how it happened!' I say.

'Oh?' she says, and I know she'd be raising an eyebrow right now if she had any.

'We were never going to *use* it,' I choke out. 'It wasn't like that at all! We weren't trying to figure out how to detonate it. We're not idiots.'

I can see Rex's face forming into a *could have fooled me* expression, but Florrie cuts in.

'But you *did* detonate it,' she says.

'OK, yes,' I say. 'But that was an accident—'

'But you did detonate it,' she says again, bluntly.

'Just part of it!' I appeal to Rex and DX-9. 'Not all of it!'

'Enough of it,' Florrie says. 'And if it hadn't been

for me, Jake Hendrick would have died.'

'OK, but,' I say, 'the point is—'

'The point is, he's still alive,' she says. 'And so are you.'

The words hang in the air for a second as I realise the subtext behind them: *Cranshaw isn't.*

That horrible realisation hits me again, thundering into my veins. Human or unit, it was my fault that bomb detonated and Cranshaw was killed. I feel the corners of my mouth twitch downwards, and I meet Florrie's eyes again. She's still staring right at me. Is that hurt somewhere down in the bright blue? She looks so much more human than I ever realised.

'I . . .' I start to say, my voice loud in the perfectly still room. I don't even know what I'm about to say. Sorry? To Florrie? For Cranshaw's death?

'But this isn't about what happened at Oaktree,' she says abruptly. 'This is about now. What's happening with us housebots and the . . .' she looks over the three of us, one at a time, 'rest of you.'

'With the *free* units, you mean,' Rex interjects.

Florrie waves a hand airily, and for a second the gesture is so absolutely human I feel my stomach tilt with nausea. It's almost nostalgic, in a horrible, completely wrong way.

'Millie,' she's saying.

'What?'

'I need to know,' she says.

'What do you need to know?' I say, the fear creeping with quick fingers up the back of my neck. I'm starting to feel claustrophobic in here, like the air's too thick to breathe.

'At Oaktree, you didn't know you were a unit,' she says.

It's a statement, not a question. But I attempt to answer anyway.

'No, I only found out when Dr Tavish told me . . .' I start, then notice Rex and DX-9 turning to look at me.

'I mean,' I stumble, 'I only have his word for it. I know I thought it was true at first, but then I started to think about it—'

'You didn't like units,' Florrie says over me.

My face flushes. It's really quite hot in here. 'Er, I . . .' I begin, but can't go on. My words just hang awkwardly in the air. Everyone looks at me. I can't meet DX-9's gaze.

'I didn't know what was going on!' I burst out. 'People I knew were disappearing! What was I meant to think? Someone was attacking pupils on school grounds! Anyone would have thought the same.'

'And you thought it was us,' she says.

'I didn't know!' I say.

'You accused me in public after your friend was found,' she says. And something about it, about her completely expressionless tone, makes me want to hit her.

'Oh, just shut up!' I say, the rage flaring suddenly and instantly within me. How dare she talk about what happened with Lu? How dare she talk about *that day*? There's a tablet and a box of spare wires on her desk. Impulsively I reach over and sweep them all to the floor with a crash. Rex and DX-9 jump up. Florrie doesn't move an inch, but her eyes flicker.

'Please,' she says, steely, 'don't do that again.'

Rex grips my shoulder. In my ear he mutters, 'If you ruin this for me . . .'

I squirm away from him. I don't care. I don't care about your stupid agreement with the housebots or your stupid revolution or stupid, stupid units. But, limply, I allow him to steer me into a chair. My teeth are gritted so hard I can feel my temples shaking. I fold my arms. One more thing. If she says just one more thing, I'm storming out. I'm getting out of here, away from the others, and I'm tracking down Company headquarters.

'I told you,' Florrie says, sounding as grim as I feel. 'I need to know the truth from you.'

'What truth?' I snap.

'Why you've decided to take up this role, with the units,' she says.

I look up at her, my mind blank.

'Before, you didn't like units,' she says, as if speaking to an idiot. 'We knew it, and we knew why.'

I open my mouth to say something, something like, 'You didn't know anything and you don't know anything now!' But I don't. I just kind of gormlessly gawp at her.

'It was obvious you didn't know what you were,' she continues.

I can feel the anger boiling up in me again. I want to retort, '*What* am I then?'

'A moment ago you were talking about your brother.

171

Clearly you still care for him,' Florrie carries on, 'but you want to lead the units against the humans? You can't still believe humans are your family, with what you've got planned?'

'I do, of course I do,' I say. 'Of course they're still my family!'

For half a second Florrie loses her composure and her face drops, totally exasperated.

'I don't want to hurt humans!' I say. 'I've always said that!'

Rex's hand is on my shoulder again, jolting me so hard my bones grind together. 'She's just . . . confused,' he says hurriedly.

Florrie ignores him. 'But you want to help units, at any cost?' she says to me.

'No, God no!' I say, flabbergasted. 'Not at *any* cost!'

'What?' Florrie says. And her eyes slowly travel over to Rex.

'Millie . . .' he says threateningly.

'I won't hurt humans,' I say. 'Whatever you say, I am not going to hurt anyone.'

Florrie glares at me for a long moment, looking like she's chewed on a wasp.

'What was the point of this, Rex?' she says, though she's still looking at me. 'You said she was ready.'

'I . . .' Rex is hesitant. It's the first time I've ever seen him like this. 'I – There may have been a misunderstanding. What I meant was—'

172

'You said she was even more militant than you are,' Florrie says, her voice sounding like ground glass.

'She is!' Rex says. 'She just doesn't know it yet.' They're both looking over me now, like I can't hear them.

'Hey!' I say.

Florrie ignores me. 'She looks exactly like she did when she left school.'

'That's not true,' I say. 'I've got . . . purple hair now . . .'

'You said she was halfway to peeling the skin off her own face and embracing her unit-hood,' Florrie says.

'Ugh,' I say.

'She's a bit squeamish about blood still, but she'll come round!' Rex says. 'Look.' And suddenly he jerks towards me. I block him with my forearm.

'Get away from my face!' I shout.

'Come on, Millie!' he says pleadingly, from beneath my arm.

'Look, I'm sorry,' Florrie says, shaking her head, 'but you don't exactly seem unified . . .'

'We are!' Rex yelps. Then, in an undertone to me, 'Just say we are, idiot.'

'You can't have a unit who sympathises with humans front and centre of your movement,' Florrie says. 'How's that going to look?'

Rex has gone a funny puce colour. The metal underneath his ripped cheek glints.

'Housebots aren't going to follow a wishy-washy leadership that doesn't know what direction it's going in,'

173

Florrie's saying. 'We have *principles*.'

'Yeah? Really?' Rex barks, sounding more like the Rex I know. 'Why haven't you joined the rest of us then?'

There's a beat of silence, in which DX-9's palm meets its face. Florrie's eyes brighten. 'Because housebots don't want to end up sitting around in an old shopping centre for weeks on end when we could be working!'

'Working for the enemy!' Rex yells. 'Keeping your unit brethren on society's lowest rung while you suck up to the fleshbags . . .'

'Wait a minute . . .' I say.

'At least we're not festering in our own bitterness!' Florrie retorts.

'We've been planning our next step, not blithely taking bribes from humans in exchange for a sham of a job!' Rex spits back.

'Leadership?' I say, finally catching on to what Florrie said. 'You wanted *me* to lead the units against the humans?'

Rex looks at me blankly and for a second I expect him to deny it.

'That's what I *told* you!' he says at the top of his voice.

'No, you didn't!' I shout back. 'You said . . . you said . . .' But with everything that's happened, I'm scrabbling to remember what he *did* say.

'You're the world's most dangerous unit, for pity's sake,' Rex says. 'Or at least, the humans think you are.'

'I thought . . .' I try to marshal my thoughts. 'I thought you meant more like a figurehead . . .'

Rex's jaw tightens.

'Or . . . a mascot,' I finish lamely.

Florrie has been watching the whole exchange.

'She doesn't even know?' she says.

'There's just been a bit of miscommunication!' Rex bites back at her. 'She gets it now.'

'Do you even want units to have more power?' Florrie asks me, her laser-blue eyes burning into mine.

My mind is instantly wiped blank and for a second all I can do is open my mouth and gawp at her like a fish.

'Well?' she says. Rex and DX-9 are looking at me, waiting. Even the other housebot, who I'd forgotten was in the room, is craning its neck to look over at me.

'Yes,' I say, after too long a pause. 'I mean, of course . . .'

'And you're willing to fight against humans to achieve this?' Florrie says, offering me another chance to say what she wants me to.

I can see Rex and DX-9 urging me with their eyes to say yes.

But units fighting humans. I just keep seeing Florrie, on the school grounds at Oaktree on that awful night, crushing Jake's throat into the ground. Units are so much stronger than humans, it's not even really a question of 'fight'. And they don't need food and they don't bleed and they can't be stopped by force alone. If they decide to destroy us, humanity is finished.

Everyone's still looking at me.

'The thing is, I don't think I am a unit after all,

and . . . and I know I've been living with units and stuff, because I didn't have anywhere else to go, because . . . because of the police chasing me and stuff, I was desperate and it's not that I don't think units should be treated fairly, because I do, now, even if I didn't before—'

'What? What did you just say?' Florrie is boggling at me.

'I mean, I'm human,' I say. 'I've been human all this time. I am human. Someone got it wrong somewhere. I'm human.'

'You mean, you were constructed to live as a human, don't you, Millie?' Rex says loudly over me.

I shake my head. 'No. I am human.'

'You're not,' Florrie says.

I look right back at her. 'I am.' My voice is steady; I'm more sure of myself now I've said it.

'No, believe me,' she says. 'You are, most definitely, one hundred per cent unit.'

I jump up. 'Explain this then,' I say, pulling my hair up around my neck to show her the still red cut on my jawline.

Her eyes flick down to it, but no other part of her face moves.

'How . . . ?' Florrie is shaking her head. 'I don't understand how you can bleed.'

'Well, I did,' I say, still thrusting my jaw at her.

'You're not human,' Florrie says to me bluntly.

I don't flinch.

'Prove it,' I say to her.

176

Her eyes dart around. I'm not sure if she's actually looking around for a solution. My mind flashes back to Rex trying to force the knife into my hand. I probably shouldn't push her to find proof. I stick my chin out to cover up the wobble in my bravado.

'You're not,' she says finally. 'There's just too much to explain.'

'Not really,' I say. I don't actually like to think about it too hard. The point is, I'm human and that's it. 'Obviously someone just got mixed up somewhere and there was another unit on the Oaktree grounds last summer.'

'There wasn't,' Florrie says.

The bluntness of her tone is getting on my nerves. 'How do *you* know?' I snap. 'You didn't know anything at the time.'

Florrie gives me a look. 'We all knew you were a unit.'

I roll my eyes. 'Yeah, right,' I say. 'A human pupil returns to school as a unit no one else knows about, then other children start going missing, and you just – what? – don't say anything? Just wait and see how it's going to turn out? You couldn't have known.' My memory unhelpfully presents me with the image of Florrie staring into my eyes in the world-culture exam and I push it away.

'We don't report on our own,' Florrie says in an ice-cold voice.

I ignore that. 'Look, I know you're cross because this wrecks your whole plan, but that's really not my fault,' I say. 'I am human, and I can't be expected to lead a

177

revolution of units against my own kind.'

'I told you, she's impossible,' Rex mutters to DX-9.

'You said she was ready for leadership,' Florrie snaps. 'You said she hated humans.'

'Stop talking about me like I'm not here!' I yell.

'There is one way we could make her see,' Florrie says slowly.

'What?' I say.

'How?' Rex says. 'I tried to cut her already, and that totally backfired.'

'Like this,' Florrie says. She holds up her index finger, which has a flat oval tip. Slowly the edge begins to glow red, spreading out until her whole fingertip is burning, sizzling and smoking.

'What is that?' I say, taking a step away.

'Maybe we shouldn't do this,' DX-9 says from the door.

'Shut up,' Rex says. 'What will it do?' There's a relish in his voice that I do not like at all.

'If she's human . . .' Florrie says, advancing towards me.

'. . . Which she's not,' Rex says hurriedly.

'If she's human,' Florrie repeats, 'the smell of burning flesh will be unmistakable.'

'No!' I shriek. How can she say it so casually, as if she's talking about burning toast?

'Just hold still, Millie,' Florrie says, reaching for me.

'Get off!' I say, smacking her arm away. I stumble backwards, tripping over the chair, and Florrie and Rex are suddenly practically on top of me.

'No!' I yell again, kicking at them and scrabbling away from Florrie's red-hot metal claw. I make it to the door.

DX-9 is there, and for a second I think it's going to block my way. But at the last moment it steps aside and suddenly I'm in the kitchen.

There's steam everywhere, with stressed-looking housebots bobbing around like croutons in a soup. I dart across the room towards the swing doors, knocking a metal table with my hip.

'Hey! Where do you think you're going?' A housebot has spotted me. 'You can't go out there!'

I whip past it and barrel towards the doors, just as another housebot elbows through them with a tray balanced on each forearm.

We smash into each other. The trays drop to the floor with an eardrum-bursting sound. Half-eaten canapés splatter all over the door frame. But I don't pause for a second. I duck under the housebot's arm and into the hall.

It's so crowded with humans that for a moment I'm completely disorientated. I wheel around, jittery with adrenaline. There's a long trestle table to the left of me, covered with a white tablecloth and serving platters of food. The swing doors behind me clatter open and I dive underneath the table before the housebots can spot me.

I crawl as far away from the kitchen as possible, then sit on the carpet and try to slow my breathing down. My heart is galloping along like it's in a race and I can't get Florrie's smile out of my head. At least my skin's still intact, and I got away from the units. Now I just need to get to Company headquarters.

I can see dozens of human legs along the full length of the table. People filling up their plates, their shiny shoes sticking underneath the hem of the tablecloth. I can hear talking. It takes my ears a moment to adjust to the human voices; I'm so used to hearing units talk now that the dips and rises of human conversation, not to mention their accents, sound strange.

'I couldn't live in a house on the moon, darling,' a man is saying, his conker-shiny brown brogues pointing right at me, as he leans over the table. 'No fresh salmon fillets available up there.'

'Well, they won't be for much longer down here either,' a woman's nasal voice replies. 'The Company's only farm is pretty much on its last legs. You'll have to settle for salmon-flavoured mudge soon either way.'

'Oh God, I can't abide that stuff, it tastes like rancid fish guts,' the man says. 'But that's not the only thing. I mean, it doesn't exactly offer stunning views, does it? Unless you want to look at nothing but a giant rotating planet for eternity. And the oxygen is pumped in from a machine – is that even healthy?'

'It's fine,' the woman says, shifting her weight from one black suede ankle boot to the other. 'And you have to remember, the whole point of having a base there is for emergencies. We all know that people who move up there permanently don't have the best quality of life.'

'Yah, yah,' the man agrees.

'But that's not what we're suggesting,' the woman smoothly continues. 'This would simply be a disaster -response base. An extra headquarters, equipped with everything we would need, available as a refuge to all higher-ranking employees, in the event of an emergency on earth.'

The man snorts. 'But what emergency could be that bad?'

I hear a housebot walk past. I jolt, crawling on my knees further up the table, my heart hammering against my ribcage again. I peek out from under the tablecloth; there aren't any units around as far as I can see. But, to my surprise, there's a little group of vaguely familiar-looking people standing nearby. They're all dressed identically in sky-blue outfits with matching sky-blue shoes. I whip back under the tablecloth, sweat prickling the back of my neck. They're Oaktree pupils. But why would they be here?

As if hearing my thoughts, an adult voice pipes up above me.

'Why are there children here?' The voice is gruff and middle-aged-sounding. I have a feeling this man has a beard.

'I don't know,' another man, with a higher, reedier voice replies. 'The PR team thought it would look good, I suppose.'

'Look good?' the gruff man snorts, as a woman says, 'It's a bit more than that!'

'No, I know, the whole "next generation" thing,' the

181

reedy-voiced man says. 'I know they keep saying that by 2120 all our business will take place up there, and today's children will be tomorrow's citizens of the moon, but that's just—'

'That's not all,' the woman says. 'They'll have to open a school up there at some point, and the Oaktree pupils are here to represent the Company's best and brightest.'

'They've eaten all the cream cakes,' the gruff-voiced man says.

'Well, all they usually get to eat is mudge . . .' the woman starts, defensively. As I near the end of the table, I realise it's right next to a doorway. If that door leads to the outside . . . Suddenly a mini-quiche rolls under the tablecloth, right in front of me. I freeze.

'Oh, I dropped one,' a voice says from above. A man's silhouette crouches behind the tablecloth, and suddenly an arm is reaching underneath, right next to me. I stay absolutely still. The hand – the human hand, a giant gold watch across the wrist, the nails expertly manicured – gropes around the dark red carpet, slowly inching towards me.

'For pity's sake, leave it, Derek,' a woman's voice sounds from above. 'There are about a million of them.'

The hand retreats and I let out a long breath.

'I wanted that one though,' the man's voice says, as he stands up. 'All the rest look a bit squished, and is that dirt on this one?'

'I don't know,' the woman says. 'The catering isn't what it used to be.'

182

'I don't know why they just can't tinker with the housebots so they can cook,' the man grumbles. 'I had to choke down a steak the other night that was medium-well.'

There's a pause as a young voice interrupts them. 'Ooh, more cream cakes!' A pair of sky-blue shoes pokes under the table as an Oaktree pupil reaches between the two adults. As soon as she's gone, they start talking again.

'So, not teaching manners at the school any more, I imagine,' the man says.

'Oh, don't,' the woman says. 'They've had an awful time recently. The Company's going to have to spend a packet on therapy in about five years.'

'Awful time?' the man half guffaws. 'What, did the shopping centre close down? Did the mudge machine break?'

The woman pauses. 'No, their head teacher died.'

My skin goes cold.

The man, who must have been taking a sip of his drink, chokes. 'Oh, oh yes, sorry,' he says. 'I forgot. Who's in charge there now?'

'I think they're just carrying on without her,' the woman says. 'Muddling along until a permanent replacement is arranged.'

'Of course, of course, how awful,' the man, who sounds very uncomfortable, says. 'Gracious ... What happened again?'

'Rufus, how can you not know?' the woman snaps. 'It was all over the news for weeks. It was all to do with

183

that killerbot disguised as a pupil – you know, the Hendricks' girl.'

I can't help letting out a tiny squeak.

'Oh, *that*,' the man says. 'Well, of course I heard about that.'

The sooner I get to Company headquarters, the sooner I can explain, the sooner everyone will know I'm human, the sooner everyone will know I didn't kill anyone.

I'm virtually at the door. I make a break for it.

A pair of shoes steps into the space between the end of the table and the door. A familiar pair of shoes. Unlike all the other shoes I've seen tonight, they're not polished to a shine brighter than the sun or made of suede softer than a kitten's ear. They're just ordinary, with slightly scuffed toes. And I used to see them in debate class at Oaktree twice a week for an hour.

The feet and the tweed-trousered legs don't move.

'Only one cream cake, Violet,' a voice suddenly says. Every inch of my skin prickles into goose pimples. I know that voice. *Welbeck*.

I'm not ready for this. I can't have an impromptu reunion with Oaktree's scariest teacher right now. But the door is right there, if only he'd move out of the way for a second.

But he's not budging. Of course he's not, it's Welbeck. As if he'd miss the chance to monitor everyone's buffet consumption.

Slowly, slowly, I pull back the tablecloth by half an

184

inch. Welbeck's looking over the table with that hawk-like expression he gets when he's preparing to tell someone off. Behind him is a huge screen, stretching halfway around the wood-panelled room, filled with the Company logo: a leaf inside a circle. I haven't seen it in so long. My stomach sinks with a yearning for the days I saw it everywhere I looked. Back then, it barely even registered. It just meant I was at home.

But the Company logo isn't the only thing on the screen. It's superimposed on to an image of the moon's landscape, with houses in silhouette. As I watch, the image changes to a giant building – no, development – growing out of the horizon, dwarfing everything else. The Company logo swoops down on to it.

A nearby woman watching turns to the woman next to her. 'You know they're only making a big deal out of this because the other companies are merging,' she says casually, and drinks an entire flute of champagne in one gulp.

'Oh, I didn't know that was official yet,' the other woman says, in a way that shows she didn't know about it at all.

'I told you they tried to headhunt me, right?' the first woman says. Welbeck sighs and strides across the room, away from the two women. This is my chance. Now. I need to go, but I don't, because across the room Welbeck has interrupted a conversation.

My stomach realises who they are before my brain catches up: something about the way they're standing, the girl's chestnut-coloured hair, the boy's stringy physique (even taller than I remember) makes my insides explode. It's Riley and Jake. They look just the same, yet totally different. Riley is enthusiastically nodding at something Welbeck's saying, while Jake's eyes are roaming around, bored. He's holding a plate with about five cream cakes, and he pushes one into his mouth, whole.

I duck back under the table. This is too weird a coincidence. They should be at Oaktree, I should be in an abandoned shopping centre in east London somewhere, but we're not. We're both here, in the same place, at the same time. *Is* this is a weird coincidence? Or have I finally had a bit of luck?

I can either make a run for it now, take my chances in the city and hope I don't get caught before I find Company headquarters, or I can talk to Jake. Jake, my twin brother, who loves units, who has always loved units – at least until this summer – and who is about the only human in the world that might actually listen to me. And believe me.

Might.

But to reach Jake, I have to cross the room.

My heart is thumping harder than ever. I pull my hood over my hair and slide slowly out from under the table. Throughout the room, metal glints between human bodies. The units have spread out, looking for me.

I dash forward, hiding behind a large group of adults talking about the economy. Squeezing between shirt-straining bellies, I slip through the crowd, aiming for

Welbeck's head. I keep expecting one of the humans to ask what I'm doing here, but their eyes skim over me, uninterested. I duck between three men talking loudly about a new Company policy they think is really great. They ignore me, but a housebot suddenly pops up on the other side, looking right at me. It moves towards me, holding a tray. I'm about to just give up on subtlety and run across the room when the three men notice the unit.

'Food's not really up to much nowadays, is it?' one of them says as they surround it.

'I was saying earlier – can't they just change them?' another man says. 'Fiddle around with their brains or something?'

The unit's eyes haven't left me, but it can't get past. I move away, keeping my head down, and then the crowd opens up and I can see Jake and Riley right ahead of me.

At the edge of my vision, there's another glint. I trip over my own feet in my haste to get away.

A woman in a green ballgown turns as I try to squeeze past her. 'Oh, look, there's a unit there,' she says, and suddenly, miraculously, a group of humans descends on the housebot, before it can get to me.

'Are there any more cream cakes in the kitchen?' one man is saying.

'My canapé has broken glass in it!' a woman says.

'You know, these salmon ones would really be improved by some dill,' someone else calls out.

I spin away from them, and bang straight into Riley.

She's standing alone now.

'Riley!' I say, breathless.

She turns round, a plate in her hand – and her whole face drops.

'It's me,' I say.

Her mouth falls open, displaying a not inconsiderable amount of cream cake.

'Riley,' I say, almost wanting to shake her, 'where's Jake gone? I need to know.'

She's frozen. Her eyes are getting wider and wider. At this rate they're going to drop out of her head.

'Riley, please, help me,' I say, my voice keening with desperation. And for a split second her eyes flick left. To a sign on the wall that points down a corridor to the toilets.

But before I can even take it in, Riley takes a big breath and screams, 'Help!'

Every human and unit in the room turns to us. Riley screams again, and this time she doesn't stop. The room becomes a wall of shocked human faces.

Then suddenly the wall comes alive. The room snaps into action, people reel backwards, yelling, 'Call the police!' and, 'It's her!'

I dash to the corridor and barge through the door to the boys' bathroom.

Jake is washing his hands. He jumps about a foot in the air, spraying water everywhere, as I slam the door shut behind me. The only way to lock it is with a chip, and I don't have one. I brace myself against it instead.

'Look, Jake,' I say. I feel as though I spend my life in other people's toilets lately. Although this is a much posher one than the one in the Humans First building, it's still a *boys'* one.

'Don't come any closer!' he yells, his voice verging on hysterical. He's backed right up against the window, as if he might jump out.

'Jake,' I start again, 'there's been a mistake. I don't know how, I'm still not sure. But what everyone's been saying – what the news has been saying about me – they're wrong.'

Jake's face doesn't move.

'I'm human,' I say. 'I'm not a unit.'

Still no reaction. There's a bang on the door behind me.

'Cut me and I bleed,' I say. 'Look!' And I pull my hair back again, to show him the scar. But he just looks back at me blankly. I can't tell what he's thinking.

'Jake, do you understand what I'm saying?' I say. The banging on the door is getting louder, and more forceful. I put my arms against the door frame.

'Jake!' I say. 'Say something!'

'I know what you're going to do,' he says.

'Huh?' I say as the door shakes.

'You're just waiting to explode,' he says, 'aren't you?'

'No, Jake!' I say. 'Didn't you listen? Don't you believe me?'

'Stop trying to trick me!' he yells. 'I know what you are!'

'I'm your sister!' I yell back.

'My sister was killed!' he says, spit flying out of his mouth. 'She's been dead for months!'

His voice is so loud it's hurting my ears. His face is screwed up in anger now, and fear. I feel my body drop with shock and the door smashes open behind me. Two police officers burst into the bathroom. They grab me by an arm each. I try to wriggle away, but one of them catches me and slams me painfully against the door frame.

'Jake!' I choke out. 'Help me!'

But he's gone.

One of the police officers is holding my wrists at the wrong angle, fumbling around for handcuffs, while the other has his forearm crushing into the back of my shoulders. A tear trickles out of the corner of my eye.

The first officer has finally found his cuffs.

'Will those work on . . . it?' the second one says in a low voice. 'Considering what it's capable of?'

He takes a tentative step away from me, slightly loosening his hold on my shoulders, and I slide to the floor. They both watch me as I slump against the wall, crying.

'Trust me,' the first one says to the second in a slightly less confident voice. He pulls out my wrist, holding up the handcuffs –

And suddenly his whole body tenses, jerking around as he yelps with pain then slumps forward on the floor, out cold. Rex is standing behind him.

'Hey!' The other one has barely taken in what's happened when Rex electrocutes him too, jabbing at him with his finger.

'How – how –' I'm still half sobbing, half hiccupping. 'How did you do that?'

'Easy,' Rex shrugs. He shows me his finger. The skin-and-metal tip is cracked open and several copper wires are hanging out, sparking when they touch.

'Did–did you just do that?' I say, wiping tears away from my face. 'Like, just now?'

'Yeah,' he says. 'I'll get it fixed back up at the shopping centre.' He holds out a hand to help me up, but I don't take it.

'Why did you save me?' I say.

'Have we really got time to talk about that?' he says. 'The police are everywhere. They've spread out but they'll be on us in seconds.'

'Then how are we going to escape?' I say. 'If we can't get back to the kitchen—'

'I've got a plan,' Rex says, with a smug smile.

He guides me over to the window and wrenches it open. I crawl out on to the sill. It's freezing outside and I can see my breath, heaving out in white clouds.

'There's no way we can jump from here,' I say. We're at least five floors up, above a cold unyielding pavement, and there's no DX-9 around to help us out.

'I know,' says Rex condescendingly. 'This way.' He pulls himself up, by the guttering, on to the building's slate roof. He holds his hand down and I grab it, though I'm not one hundred per cent sure he'll be able to take my weight.

191

But somehow I scramble up next to him, the cold of the slates seeping through my clothes. We sit with our feet in the gutter.

'What was your plan then?' I say.

Rex is silent. I lean over, looking at the pavement below.

'If DX-9 were here, it'd just jump,' I say.

'Look, shut up,' Rex says. 'I'm trying to think.'

I start to shiver, feeling as though the cold night air is sinking directly into my bones and my blood. The stars aren't as bright here as they were at Oaktree. But the whole of London is lit up, like a giant patterned carpet of stars laid in front of us. All the buildings, all the cars on the street, every single window, seems to blaze with light. I take a big deep breath.

There's a huge shiny silver building almost directly in front of this one, a few streets over, which looks vaguely familiar. Then it clicks: Company headquarters. It's right there. It's been this close all along. If I could just get down to the street –

But the street below is filling up with police cars, sirens caterwauling. As we watch, a huge police van pulls up and loads more officers get out.

'We're trapped here, aren't we?' I say.

Rex pauses. 'Yes,' he says.

The silence thumps between us like a heartbeat. The seconds of my last moments of freedom counting down. Rex is fidgeting beside me, chewing his fingernails. There are sounds below us now, in the bathroom. I take another big breath of cold air and almost feel calm. It's going to happen now. At least I don't have to run any more.

And then DX-9's head pops out from the other side of the pointed roof.

'Are you two going to make, like, any attempt to escape *at all*?' it says.

'Where did you come from?' I squeak, as we clamber up the slates.

'The kitchen,' says DX-9. '*I* never left.' There's a subtle emphasis on the *I* that I ignore. In fact, I'm so relieved to see DX-9 I almost attempt to hug it – but realise our location makes that a bit impractical.

'Quickly now,' DX-9 says. We climb into the opposite gutter, and without taking a breath DX-9 slides smoothly down the drainpipe and into the courtyard.

Rex and I share a look.

'Come on then,' it calls from down below.

'You first,' Rex says.

'No, you first,' I say.

'Oh, for crying out loud, the police are behind us, just go,' he snaps, and to even my surprise, I do. Without thinking, I hold the drainpipe, squeeze my knees around it and slide, slightly more bumpily than DX-9, down to the courtyard. Rex follows behind.

Thirteen

It's only when we're back at the shopping centre that Rex starts telling me off.

'That was our only chance to make allegiances with the housebots,' he moans, 'and you ruined it.'

'You are ridiculous,' I say. He's having his finger mended by a cleanbot who's trying to pretend not to listen to our conversation. 'Can't you just be happy we're alive? And not in prison?'

'Units don't really die,' he says. 'We just power down.'

'Not really the point,' I say.

'I can't believe how badly that meeting went,' he says, glowering at me.

'Well, maybe you should have warned me who the meeting was with!' I say. 'Before you spring a blast from the past on me!'

I keep getting waves of shock. Florrie. Riley. Jake. *My sister was killed months ago.* I can't think about it without flinching, as if it's a slap.

'I thought the worst thing that would happen would be that they'd get worried about your battery failing,' he grumbles. 'And then you go and tell them you think you're human! I mean—'

'I am human,' I say automatically.

'You're deluded,' he says.

'Can we not start this argument again?' DX-9 says.

'Did they ever finish that new skyscraper?' the cleanbot working on Rex's finger suddenly pipes up. 'The Splinter?'

Something jolts in my memory. 'Er, I don't know,' I say to it, turning to Rex. 'What was your plan with the Splinter?'

'What?' he snaps, probably a bit surprised at the drastic change of conversation topic.

'You had that model and everything,' I say. 'What is it? What is "plan B"?'

'OK . . . you know how I said we're not going to blow anything up,' Rex says. 'Well, we might let people *think* we're going to blow things up.'

'Huh?' I say.

He looks at me properly. 'Have you actually been watching any of the news about the Splinter, or have you just been switching over to find stuff about yourself?'

I open my mouth to protest. Then close it again.

'Thought so,' he says with a grin that's more of a grimace. 'The Splinter has been built because of the merger of two of the world's biggest companies. Together they make up a super-corporation.'

'Right,' I say.

'And the Splinter, their new headquarters, will be officially opened in a giant gala ceremony on New Year's Eve. The turn of the century. Every important fleshbag in the world will be there. And everyone who's not there will be watching it on TV.'

'OK, OK,' I say. 'And so, what, you're going to try and gatecrash it?'

'No,' he says, annoyed. 'We're going to hijack the whole thing.'

'OK,' I say. 'Why?'

'Why?' Rex says. '*Why?* Those companies – *all* companies – were built on the backs of units. They wouldn't be where they are now without exploiting units for the last fifty years. And now we have the right to equal treatment, equal pay and dignity, they cast us aside?' His voice echoes around the room; his face is bright red.

I lean away slightly. Yes, but not you, I think. You weren't working. You were being doted on hand and foot by your parents. You're angry about your parents, that's what this is. But I don't say it. I don't say anything.

'All we have to do is make a show of strength at the Splinter's opening, and the housebots will come running to join us,' Rex is saying. 'We have to show them what you can do.'

'What *I* can do?' I say.

'Yes!' Rex snaps. 'You're the one the humans are worried about! The most human-like robot, the one that fooled them, the walking weapon. You're the one the housebots were, until last night, interested in getting behind! If you go out there on New Year's Eve, in front of the world, and prove your strength and your power—'

'But I can't do anything!' I shout. 'I wouldn't even know *how* to make a show of strength!'

'Leave that to us,' DX-9 says gently. 'You won't have to do a thing.'

'But . . .' I'm starting to panic now. 'I don't want anyone to get hurt! It's not even anything I can do; it's just the device they think I have.'

'Them knowing we have you will be enough,' Rex says. 'They won't risk their hides deliberating. Once they've seen you, they'll give in.'

'What . . .? What about the people who think I'm human?' I say. 'They won't be scared.'

'Who? No one thinks you're human,' Rex scoffs. 'Everyone knows it's just a ploy by your Company. Everyone except *you*.'

I swallow my hurt down before it shows on my face. I don't care. It doesn't matter what Rex thinks. I know what I am.

'Well, I don't know if I *want* to help you destroy humanity,' I hit back. 'I meant what I said to Florrie.'

Rex slams his fist down on the desk. The cleanbot flinches.

197

'Learn which side you are on,' he shouts. 'You don't get to choose to be human.'

'I get to choose if I want a part in this plan or not!' I yell back.

'You. Are. A *unit*,' he booms.

'Even if I was, that's not the point!' I say. 'My Company, my family—'

'So? They have no connection to you! They hate you! You only think they're your family because some fleshbag's memories were downloaded into your brain!'

'I'm not going to help you hurt people!' I say.

'You'd let units suffer but not humans?' he shouts. 'You'd stand by and watch while units disintegrate and humans make more money?'

'I didn't say that!' I shout back. 'Just because I don't want humans hurt doesn't also mean I want units to . . . to disintegrate! Why can't everyone just . . . get along?'

Rex looks at me, disgusted. 'Live in the real world, for crying out loud, Millie.'

'No,' I say, folding my arms. 'It's horrible.'

There's a pause while we glower at each other, like fighting cats.

'Rex, remember what we talked about,' DX-9 says quietly.

'No.'

'Come on.'

'She should want to do it for the right reasons,' Rex says.

'What are you talking about?' I say.

198

'If you agreed to help us with our plan,' DX-9 says, 'Rex could message the Company and help you get back to them.'

'What?' My heart shoots up like a firework. 'You could do that?'

Rex folds his arms and scowls at DX-9. '*Only* when we're in central London,' he says, without looking at me. 'And only *after* we've achieved our goals!'

'Really?' I say, almost leaning forward to hug him, despite it being him.

'*If* I can get a signal,' he says. 'They're going to kick you straight back out—'

'Would you agree to the plan if Rex promised to do that?' DX-9 asks.

I remember all those fears I had about the units taking over. Destroying humanity. Killing humans. And now, what, I'm going to be the one leading them into battle? Against the people I spent thirteen years of my life with?

As much as I want to be back in the Company, I can't let that happen.

'If I don't do it, what will you do?' I ask, hoping they'll say they can use the second most dangerous unit in the world instead. And, as they'd be doing it either way, it won't matter if I'm the one who does it and I can go home afterwards.

'Then we can't do it,' Rex says. 'Unit power crumbles and the fleshbags win. *Again*.'

'Oh,' I say, realising I don't want that either. 'I don't know!'

'Just do it,' Rex says through gritted teeth. 'We get power, you get to be back with your lame Company.'

'It's not that simple,' I cry.

'It *is* that simple!'

'Stop it, both of you,' DX-9 says. 'Millie, will you think about it? Stay for a bit longer and consider it?'

'If she's not going to jump at the chance, then she doesn't deserve—' Rex starts, but DX-9 holds a hand up. And, miraculously, he shuts up.

'OK,' I say. 'I'll think about it.'

'You need to decide before New Year's Eve,' Rex snaps. 'And don't talk about it with everyone. I want them all focused on their own part. Loose lips sink ships.'

'Huh?' I say. 'What ships?'

'It's from World War Two,' he says. 'It's a famous slogan! Didn't they teach you anything at that school?'

In the following days, the visit to the town house starts to seem like a frantic, colourful burst of activity in a long landscape of flat dull mediocrity. The memory starts to take on a shimmering, dream-like quality, and as much as I tell myself, I came face-to-face with Riley. I spoke to Jake. It all really happened, it feels as detached and far away as if I watched the whole thing on TV.

The only thing that still pierces me like a knife are Jake's words: 'My sister was killed! She's been dead for months!'

I try not to think them at all, but they keep repeating, over and over again, in my dreams, rising up from nowhere.

Rex doesn't speak to me again, just curls his lip if he passes by me, until an afternoon a few days later.

I'm watching TV footage of human workers installing fairy lights up and down the Splinter when Rex bends down to my ear.

'You need to decide,' he says. 'Yes or no? We leave for central London in less than twenty-four hours.'

I nibble at my fingernails, not looking at him.

'Well?' he says.

'I haven't decided yet,' I say.

'Still?' he half barks. I shift away from him.

'If you don't help, we stay here, we make no progress, and you continue to have the threat of the police bursting in and arresting you hanging over you at every moment,' he reels off.

'Look, it's not an easy decision,' I say.

A muscle is twitching in Rex's jaw, just under his wound. 'We need an answer. Soon. You've had enough time.'

After he stalks off, I sit on the floor with my head leaning against the Spend 'n' Vend's glass panel, cramming rainbow-coloured glitter dust into my mouth on autopilot. Every time I finish a packet the Spend 'n' Vend dispenses another one. The screenbot next to me is showing the New Year's Eve preparations in London on loop. I watch without seeing, my glitter-stained fist going from packet to mouth, packet to mouth, packet to mouth.

The screenbot flashes up a question over a helicopter shot of London. *So . . . are you going to . . .*

'I don't know,' I say out loud. My tongue has shrivelled up with the tangy taste of the rainbow dust. I have that same slightly sick feeling I used to get after every Winter Festival and trip to the Woodland River Centre. Something I would never have noticed the absence of in a million years. I can't believe I ever thought I had been created by a scientist in a laboratory. That they could have designed me, right down to the way my tongue reacts to different chemicals. As if Dr Tavish would have taken the time to even bother fitting me with a sense of taste, which no one else would have ever been able to check, or a fully functioning circulation system.

I'm human. There shouldn't be any maybe about it. I have a lifetime of evidence backing me up. Source: being human for thirteen years versus one half-hour in which Dr Tavish, who I have no reason to trust, told me something different. There's no good reason to believe that I'm a unit. What will happen if Rex stands up and tells the world I can detonate? The humans won't wait to check if it's real. They'll kill me. And I'll die, because I'm not made of indestructible metal.

DX-9 has zoomed up to me. 'We need you,' it says.

'Leave me,' I say, not lifting my head off the Spend 'n' Vend. 'I'm thinking.'

'There's a human in the basement,' it says.

202

This gets my attention.

'What?'

'They asked for you,' it says.

My heart is lodged somewhere in my throat as I stand up. 'A human?' Glitter dust drops off me in a rainbow-coloured cloud.

'Come now,' it says, zooming off. I follow half a step behind, my pulse drumming a tattoo in my neck. We clatter down the lift into the basement, which is full of units all standing in a circle around a chair in the middle. A chair that a human is sitting on.

It's a girl, her head bowed, blonde hair hanging down over her face. I feel a huge rush of emotion up against my eye sockets. My lips wobble. Shell. I haven't seen my best friend in such a long time, and she's suddenly in front of me. I'm about to say, 'I missed you so much,' but as she lifts her head, the words die in my throat. I'm staring into my own face.

Fourteen

It's a mirror. It must be. Yes, that's it, some kind of mirror the units set up in the basement for some reason they haven't told me about.

But even as I'm telling myself this, I can feel my jaw slackening, I know my eyebrows are in my hairline, and this girl, this other Millie, doesn't look shocked at all. She just looks angry. Her eyebrows are furrowed together and her mouth is all pinched and curled up underneath her nose.

Do *I* look as petulant when I'm angry? No wonder Rex never takes me seriously.

'So, it's you,' she says, folding her arms.

If this were a film I would fold my arms too and coolly say, 'And *you*,' back to her. But I'm far too flabbergasted.

'You're the unit who's been impersonating me,' she adds.

'I haven't been impersonating anyone,' I say.

'Doesn't look that way to me,' she says, quick as a flash.

There's a murmur from the surrounding units. I can't tell if they've taken my side or hers.

'I don't even know who you are,' I say loudly, over the noise.

But of course I do really. I just don't *want* to know.

Her face flushes red and her jaw twitches. 'I'm Millie Hendrick.'

There's a little beat of silence in which I know I should say, 'No, you're not' or, '*I'm* Millie Hendrick' or, 'You're lying', but I don't. My mouth has gone dry.

'I've been *forced* –' she practically spits this at me – 'to spend the last six months in hiding because of your little trick with Humans First, and—'

'Why?' I say.

'Because the police are looking for someone who looks exactly like me,' she says, '. . . idiot!'

'But . . .' I suddenly put the pieces together. 'How are you alive? Dr Tavish said you . . . you . . .'

'I *what*?'

'He said you were dead,' I say. 'He said you got blown up at the rally and they replaced you with me.' As I say it, I can feel a sinking sensation in my chest, descending until it lands with a bump in my shoes. *It is true.* Everything Dr Tavish said about me is true. Everything he said about the other Millie is true . . . except for the bit about her being dead.

205

I am a unit.

'Well, I didn't die,' the other Millie is saying. 'One minute I was at the rally with my brother, the next I was waking up in a rubbish-disposal unit halfway across the city with no memory of who I was or how I got there.'

She looks at me accusingly.

'Well.' I don't know what else to say.

'I had to go and live with the redundants. On the *streets*!' She pokes me in the shoulder, hard. 'Do you know what that's like?'

'Hey!' I say. 'It wasn't my fault! I didn't even know anything until the Unit Rights Act passed!'

'Yeah, that's right,' she says. 'You're a unit.'

'And?' I say. 'What's that supposed to mean?'

The other Millie looks shifty, her eyes flicking past me to the other units.

'You do what you're told,' she says.

'No, I don't,' I say. 'I spent most of my time at school breaking all the rules. I have all *your* memories, you know. I thought I was human. I thought I was you!'

Me, my mind echoes back. *I thought I was me.*

'Well, you're not,' the other Millie snaps at me.

'Yeah, I gathered that.'

She glares at me. I just kind of bemusedly blink back at her, still shocked that she exists.

Rex's voice suddenly cuts in behind me, making me jump. I'd forgotten he was there. 'Maybe we should—'

'You won't have them for much longer,' Millie says,

206

ignoring him.

'Won't have what?'

'My memories,' she says. 'As soon as you're caught and locked up, I'm taking them back.'

'*What?*' I say again. 'But that's my – my *whole brain*. I'll have to be deprogrammed.'

'So? They're not yours,' she shouts.

'But you don't need them.' I can hear my voice getting squeakier, losing control. 'You have them anyway!'

'No, I don't, not all of them!' she says. 'I don't have a chip or the ability to brainstream any more! *They* removed it all and gave them to *you*.' She holds up her finger – the tip bears a livid red gouge like a bite mark. 'I need my memories back.'

'You can't have them,' I say, clutching my face, as if that will protect me from her.

'This isn't *fair*!' she shrieks. 'I had to work all this out, you know, everything. I woke up with no memories and I had no idea who I was. It wasn't until *you* started popping up on the screens everywhere that I began to piece it together.' She looks at me like I'm the thing she hates most in the world, and I suppose I probably am.

'When I became a wanted person or you became a wanted person—'

'Unit,' Rex corrects, behind me.

'Unit,' she agrees, 'the redundants wouldn't let me be around them any more. They all got given jobs and they left me. I didn't have anywhere to go. I didn't know

207

what was going on.'

I feel smug for a fleeting moment. The units wanted me to stay. Even though it was dangerous for them.

'If you had nowhere to stay, why didn't the police catch you?' I say.

'They almost did,' she hits back. 'Millions of times. And I wouldn't even have been able to prove I wasn't a unit; everyone knows you've been able to pass human medical tests.' She pauses, looking at me dead on.

'The only way for me to get back to the Company and my family,' she adds, almost as an afterthought, 'is for you to turn yourself in.'

The units all turn their heads as one and look at me expectantly. The other Millie looks at me. Rex is looking at me. Everyone is waiting for an answer.

'I-I can't,' I say in a very small voice.

There's a clink of metal as the units all turn to look at the other Millie. For a second her lip wobbles, then she composes herself.

'You have to,' she says.

Rex suddenly steps forward, between us. 'That isn't going to happen tonight at least,' he says casually.

'Or ever,' I say, less casually. I'm trying to keep my voice steady, to show I'm in control, but it's difficult.

'I could just go to the police and say I know where you are,' the other Millie shouts at me.

'No, you couldn't. They'd lock you up before you could say anything,' I shoot back, surprised at my own venom.

There's a murmur of noise across the assembled units. They're impressed. The other Millie does a weird frustrated scream from the back of her throat.

'Do you know how hard this has been?' she says. 'Working all this out – putting everything together—'

'It's not exactly been a rose garden for m—' I start, but she interrupts.

'Suddenly my face is everywhere and I don't know why,' she rants, appealing to the units rather than me. 'I'm wanted for a crime that I not only didn't commit, but that took place somewhere I don't ever remember being—'

'You don't remember Oaktree?' I say, surprised.

Rolling lawns, wildflowers nodding in the wind across the grounds. Climbing trees and jumping off them when we were eight. Lacrosse, hockey, cross-country running. The smell of the books in the Old Section of the library. Giggling with Shell, Lu and Riley in the dormitories after lights-out. Eating mudge in the canteen, running about in the fields, units waiting on us hand and foot.

And these are not just distant memories. This was my life until six months ago.

'I remember *now*,' the other Millie is saying. 'After the news broke, things started coming back. They said a unit with my face had attacked pupils at a boarding school and I realised I already knew what it looked like. I only saw bits and pieces of the TV coverage, because I was always on the move. But I saw enough interviews with Jake and Shell to remember them.'

'Interviews?' I say, noting the plural. I've only seen that one interview. Suddenly I'm desperate to know how Shell is. My best friend. Does she hate me like Jake does? Would she react the way he did if we came face to face? 'You've seen them? How did they look?'

'That's none of your business,' she snaps.

'My best friend and my brother?' I say. 'Of course it's my business—'

'*My* brother,' the other Millie insists. 'Who you tried to kill—'

'I didn't—' I start.

'And *my* best friend—'

'You don't even remember them properly!' I say, desperate.

'Because *you've* got my memories!' she shouts over me.

'Enough!' Rex yells louder than both of us. 'Shut up!'

He gestures to the other Millie, and I work out what he means before she does. He wants her to carry on with her story. I feel a little stab of hurt that he's not dismissing her.

'Anyway,' she says, 'when I saw you on TV, at Piccadilly Circus, after you disappeared down into the drains, I knew you'd joined the units. And I knew they'd be somewhere along the tube line, somewhere no one else went. So I tracked you down and found you.' She looks up, as if expecting to be flooded with praise.

I can't resist. 'And that took you nearly six months?'

'It's not easy to move around when you're identical to a wanted criminal!' she says. 'So, if you're not going to help me . . .' She raises her eyebrows, as if I might suddenly say, Oh, actually I've changed my mind! Take my brain!

'I'm not,' I say. *I can't*.

'Then I'm going,' she says, flouncing to her feet.

'I don't think so,' Rex says.

'What?' She turns to him, confused.

'You've seen everything,' he says simply. I look over at Rex's carefully crafted model of the Splinter. And the seventeen maps of central London hanging on the wall, printed by one of the screenbots.

I look at the other Millie. Her eyes flick over the walls, the model, the other units, but there's no understanding there. She doesn't know what it means. Her face is so open, so easy to read. Are all humans like this? Do I just not remember?

'We can't just . . . let you go,' Rex says gently. He puts a hand on the other Millie's shoulder and sits her back down.

'I don't understand,' she says.

'You know too much,' he says. 'And you've just threatened to go to the police about one of us. How could we trust you?' I feel a tiny glow of gratitude towards him.

'You can't keep me prisoner here,' the other Millie says, in a small, uncertain voice.

'Can't we?' Rex says. 'Are you going to fight us? Overpower us?'

There's a muffled snigger from the assembled units, and the other Millie's colour drains. Her face is now deathly white, with pink blotches on her cheeks.

211

I automatically touch my own cheeks. Do I still get those marks when I'm upset?

She's looking to me, as if for help. But I look away. I won't – *can't* – help her.

'Now –' Rex twinkles at her like a kindly grandfather – 'what shall we call you?'

'I-I'm Millie,' she hiccups.

'I know, but we already have a Millie,' he says.

'I was Millie fir—'

'I know, I know, but she got here before you,' he says, as if it's out of his hands. 'What did you call yourself before you knew you were Millie?'

There's a long silence. 'Alisha,' she says.

'Alisha?' I say. 'As in, Alisha Atkins? The book character?' I laugh. Alisha Atkins is the main character in the Company's series of action-adventure books that absolutely everyone read. 'That's the most ridiculous thing I've ever heard!'

'They're my favourite books!' she says. Her mouth is pursed and her chin is wobbling but she stares me down. 'There were ads everywhere for the new one,' she says. 'It was one of the first things that came back to me.' She ducks her head and a single tear drips down her cheek.

'I can't believe, of all things, that's what you remember,' I say.

Was I always this emotional? I'm trying so hard to hate her, but I can't help feeling sorry for her. It's like a dead weight on my chest.

212

The Spend 'n' Vend glides up, stopping between us. It drops down a pack of crispy rosemary-and-garlic-flavour mudge. I'm about to lean down and get it when the lever catapults it into the other Millie's lap.

'Wh—' I say, my hand still outstretched. I glare at the Spend 'n' Vend's outright betrayal. The other Millie looks at the pack for a second, wipes her face and huskily says, 'Thanks.'

'Someone has to watch her,' Rex says, looking right at me.

I look behind me, then look back. 'Me?'

'Yes,' he says.

'I don't want to!' I say. Surely he must realise how weird that would be for me?

'You have to; we have to keep you both together,' he says. 'If you're walking about and she escapes, how are we going to know which is which?'

'Hello?' I say. 'My hair is purple!'

'It's not though, is it?' Rex says, rolling his eyes. 'It faded back to blonde ages ago.' And then, as if he can't resist: 'The colour your hair was designed to be.'

'Oh, shut up,' I say.

'You have to watch her; *we* have more important things to do,' he says. 'You said you didn't know whether you want to be involved. So you can spare the time.'

'Maybe I do now.' I shrug.

Rex is alert. 'You do?' He leans in close, right next to my ear. 'Have you finally realised whose side you should be on?'

213

My stomach twists. I so desperately don't want to accept what's in front of me.

'Is that a yes?' Rex says.

I twirl a strand of hair around my finger, pulling it tight until my finger turns deep red. 'It's still a maybe,' I say.

Rex exhales through his nose loudly.

'What's the absolute latest I have to decide?' I ask.

'Yesterday,' he says.

'Rex . . .' I say. 'I still . . . I don't know . . .'

He closes his eyes and takes a deep breath. 'You have until the morning,' he says. I can tell he thinks he's almost got me.

'OK, OK,' I say.

'And until then, you have to watch her,' he says.

'Rex!' I say. 'That's not fair . . .'

But I know what he's worked out. The longer I have to face off against the other Millie, the harder the whole *you're-not-really-human* message is going to hit home.

So that's how I end up sitting opposite myself in one of the abandoned shops. The other Millie glares at me, so I glare back at her. I fold my arms and she folds hers. I sigh huffily and she sighs equally huffily. I realise that if someone walked in right now they'd probably think there was a mirror in the room, just like I did. Apart from the fact that I'm wearing a bright yellow jumper one of the wardrobes produced for me that morning and she's dressed in an old stained hoodie with ragged holes in the cuffs, we're identical.

214

I don't notice how long we've been sitting in stony silence until her eyelids start drooping, and then her head lolls forward. She's asleep. I feel a hot, prickly flare of jealousy in my chest and I'm not even sure why. Why don't I do that? Her breath is snuffling in and out of her nose in an almost-snore and her mouth is open a little bit. I don't do this. I just shut down. She'll wake up with a crick in her neck, her mouth tasting stale and sleep around her eyes. When I wake up I feel exactly the same as I did before I went to sleep, like I've closed my eyes for thirty seconds.

She's human. And I'm not. Without the structure of school and other humans around me, I'm moving further and further away from even passing as human. What's going to happen to me?

After a while I have to stop watching her. I can't believe how envious I am. I'm on the brink of shaking her awake and saying, 'I sleep too, you know!'

I sit outside the shop, with my back to the glass, hugging my knees, and pretending that none of this is real. It actually works quite well until DX-9 hurries over to me.

'Aren't you supposed to be watching – er – Alisha?' it says, worried.

I narrow my eyes at it, for taking me out of my fantasy world.

'She's sleeping,' I say slowly, gesturing inside the shop. 'She can't escape without walking right past me.'

DX-9's eyes flick between the shop interior and my face. 'What if . . . ?' It trails off.

215

'What?' I snap. 'What if what?'

DX-9 pauses, like it's choosing its words carefully. 'What if she wakes up and she's scared?' it says finally.

'Why would *she* be scared?' I say. 'She came here! She wanted to find us! It's *us* who should be surprised!'

'Well . . .' DX-9 looks uncomfortable. I bet the other Millie wouldn't be able to tell. Then I realise that's not exactly a tick in the human box for me.

'She'll be fine,' I say evenly. At least I think it's evenly; I don't know why DX-9 flinches.

'It's just, you know, humans and their emotions . . .' it says. And I feel a little flicker of pain because I know it doesn't think of *me* as a human. Not a real one. 'Especially after sleep. They get confused.'

'I don't think waking up to me looming over her is going to prevent her from being scared,' I say, getting up. 'Where's the Spend 'n' Vend got to?'

DX-9 takes a half-step back from me. 'You . . . You still want to eat?' it says.

'What?' I say. There's a silence, while DX-9's eyes look anywhere but my face.

'It's just . . .' it says. 'Now you . . . Now we *know* . . .'

'I'm still the same person!' I explode. 'I didn't just eat and sleep because I was trying to convince myself I was human!'

The words hang between us in the air, too loud. I try again, about nine decibels lower.

'Just because *she's* here doesn't mean I don't get

hungry all of a sudden,' I say.

I'm actually not hungry. I just like the idea of eating something. I stalk away from DX-9, let it mind 'Alisha' for a while. I dip through the crowd of units, all of who avoid making eye contact, until I spot the Spend 'n' Vend. As I approach, it dispenses two packets of gingerbread mudge. Without looking directly at it, because I'm still cross with it for giving the other Millie food, I take them and go back to DX-9.

'I'm so sorry, Millie,' it says. 'That was rude of me.'

'It's just a normal day, OK?' I say through gritted teeth. 'Let's just watch TV. And not talk.'

We wave over a screenbot and I tear a piece of mudge off and cram it in my mouth. There's nothing about me on. It's all about the Splinter and the party, on every channel. I make the screenbot scroll through them all. I just want to find someone talking about me and how the Company thinks I'm human. Or how dangerous I am and how I might have been designed to rip a man's throat out with my teeth. Something like that.

After a while the other Millie emerges from the shop, rubbing her eyes, her face all creased with sleep. I feel another jab of jealousy. It's ridiculous – why would I want a creased face or blurry eyes or hair sticking up at the back in that stupid way. The units sitting around me and the ones just hanging around, the ones cleaning or mending and even the ones charging at the side, get up and flock towards her as soon as she comes out. She's just *that* interesting.

217

I suppose a fake human could never compare to a real human.

The Spend 'n' Vend, hovering by my side, waits maybe thirty seconds before rushing over to join the others, now in a crowd around her. I can barely even see her from here, there are so many units in the way. They're all talking at her, asking her so many questions it's almost drowning out the noise from the TV channel. *Are you hungry? Are you tired? Do you need more sleep?* Like they did when I first got here.

Only DX-9 stays next to me.

The other Millie suddenly emerges out of the crowd of units like a queen, walking towards me. They're still crowding around her like an entourage.

I still find it weird to look at her. It's like my reflection has come to life and started walking around, making mean comments about me and charming all my friends. My eyes keep automatically whipping away from her, as if they can't actually believe. That image doesn't make any sense. Don't look at it, don't look at it!

This is not on the level of having a twin. I mean, Jake and I never really looked any more alike than a normal brother and sister anyway, but the other Millie is more than a twin. She's literally my double.

Or I'm hers, a fact I still can't quite grasp.

'What's going on?' she calls out to the screenbot I'm sitting in front of. Her tone, for the first time, is *friendly*. 'What are we watching?'

'For someone who hates units, she seems awfully comfortable with them,' I say to no one. Then I remember she doesn't hate units. It was me who hated units. She just hates me.

As if on cue she seems to focus on me, sitting on the floor in front of her. We glare at each other from across the space.

'What's this?' she says, moving closer. 'The news channel?' She wrinkles her nose.

'Yes, it's what we watch,' I say as bluntly as possible.

'You can put on something else if you like,' DX-9 pipes up. 'There are loads of channels.'

'OK, look, no,' I cut across it.

'What?' it says.

'She can't just come in and change everything,' I say, folding my arms. I can't help it – I just have an urge to be as horrible as possible. 'Our refuge, our rules.'

'Refuge?' the other Millie says.

She has folded her arms too now. She's glaring at me even harder, if that's possible.

'Anyway,' I say to DX-9, 'she's our prisoner. She can't just watch TV like it's no big deal. *And*,' I add as the Spend 'n' Vend excitedly trundles up to join us, 'she shouldn't be allowed food from the Spend 'n' Vend either.'

I don't know why I'm suddenly acting so *petty*. I feel that all this – the Spend 'n' Vend, friendship with the units, even the questions about being human – is mine. And I don't want to share. Not with *her*.

219

'But –' The units making up the other Millie's entourage look at me horrified. As does DX-9.

A hysterical cleanbot near the back suddenly shouts, 'But without food, can't humans *die*?'

'She won't die!' I snap. 'It's only twenty-four hours! She'll just . . . get a bit hungry.' They were never this bothered about my battery dying out.

'I wouldn't expect *you* to understand what it's like to starve,' the other Millie says icily.

'Oh no?' I say.

'You're just a unit.'

I can tell she's instantly lost the crowd, but that doesn't matter. I jump up.

'Yeah, *now* I am,' I say, 'but I *was* a human. I used to be human.'

'No, you didn't,' she says, incredulously. 'You never were. You just thought you were. Based on memories that are rightfully mine!'

I should be coming up with something cutting. But I'm not. My brain has blanked and I'm just opening and closing my mouth like a fish.

'Well?' she says, her anger melting into confusion when I don't hit back. 'Tell me I'm wrong?'

'You're . . . you're right,' I croak. 'I am a unit.' My head suddenly feels as if it weighs a thousand kilos. 'I've always been a unit.'

She's triumphant, her whole face lit up like a light bulb. 'And that means – that means your memories . . .'

220

But her voice is drowned out by the rushing sound in my ears. It has abruptly occurred to me: why am I defending humans? My connections with Jake, Shell, my friends, my parents suddenly seem ridiculous. I'm going to all these lengths to try to protect them and find my way back to them, based on what? Someone else's memories. All humans have ever done to me – *me* me, not *her* me – is hurt me. Build me, lie to me, attack me. Hunt me down. Lock me up in prison, if they get the chance.

Why am I trying to protect them?

Something Rex said a while ago is echoing back at me: *They have no connection to you! They hate you! You only think they're your family because some fleshbag's memories were downloaded into your brain!*

My face prickles when I think of all those stupid things I said to convince myself I was human. I eat and sleep because I *need to*! It can't just be a weird hangover from six months of thinking I was human! Oh, it was probably just a *strange mindset*, a *bump on the head*, that made me see the metal underneath my skin, punch through glass in that service station, tip over a police van and run about three hundred miles! I bleed a red substance that looks like human blood – concrete proof! I couldn't jump over that wall at Humans First – even though I crashed through a second-storey window without a cut on me – so *I must be human*! It's nothing to do with the fact my battery's running itself down –

My train of thought immediately stops short. My

battery is running down. All the more reason to do it.

'We just have to work out how to transfer them without a cable or a tablet –' The other Millie is right in front of me, gabbling, her face flushed with hope.

But I look right through her.

'I've got to –' I blurt out, then turn on my heel and rush across the shopping centre. I burst into Rex's office with a bang. He's sitting with his head slumped on the desk, but jerks upright when I enter.

'Millie,' he says, doing his best to look condescending.

'I'll do it,' I say.

'What?' he says, the realisation slowly dawning in his eyes.

'I'll do it,' I say. 'Let's crush them.'

He blinks. 'Crush . . . ?'

'The humans.' I almost can't believe I'm saying it. 'Let's crush the humans.'

Fifteen

A few hours later I've changed my mind. I don't want to crush the humans. I don't want to crush anyone any more. I want to be sitting in the shopping centre, eating glitter dust and watching all this play out on TV. I want the option to change the channel.

The Splinter is huge. It reaches up so far I can't even see the very top where the peak disappears into the velvety dark sky. The open-air terrace around the ground floor has been slowly filling with people for a good couple of hours now.

I had to crouch in the sewers, just by the entrance, waiting for Rex to give me the signal – two taps on the drain cover – to come out. Rex has a contact on the *inside* – he keeps saying that in a weird low voice while tapping his nose, so I'm assuming he means one of the merged companies' units. They've given us all the entry codes, so DX-9 went in first to disable the alarm system. To prevent the humans from knowing, the system could only be shut down for short intervals, so over the past few hours units – *our* units – have been slowly trickling in, infiltrating the candlelit terrace and mixing with the partygoers.

I still don't really know the plan. Rex just kept saying, 'Mingle with the crowd. Then when I start talking and the screenbots put the spotlight on you, don't do anything. Just stand still.'

'Helpful,' I'd said.

Rex half shrugged. 'It should be enough.'

All the units – apart from the few foodbots who stayed behind at the shopping centre to guard *her* – are pretending to be staff. But I can't pass as a housebot. So I'm dressed as a guest. A guest who's about a foot and a half shorter than every other guest. I think I look the part though. One of the wardrobes produced an amazing dark red dress for me. I was worried I'd be recognised, what with my face being plastered all over the city for months and everything, but then I found out it was a masquerade ball. So a feathered burgundy eye mask covering most of my face is the perfect finishing touch.

Getting ready, my hands shook with nerves. Every time I thought about what I was going to do, my breath caught in my chest. But looking in the mirror when I was dressed, I felt happy. I looked quite grown-up.

But of course, I'm not grown-up. I never will grow up.

I'll be the same, frozen at thirteen years old forever – or until I start shutting down. And *she* will get to change and grow and become an adult. How long will it take before we don't even look that alike any more? Two years? Three?

I felt burdened with jealousy, sick with it. I had to press my fists into my cheekbones to stop myself from crying. Why couldn't *I* be the human one, and *she* be the unit? *Why why why?*

I steeled myself as we set off in the sewers for London. This was just the way things were. I couldn't do anything to change it. I had to accept I was a unit, embrace it fully and take on the role of dangerous killerbot. I wouldn't be able to bring any of my human traits with me. Waiting under the drain cover for my signal to join the party, I decided: it was time to leave my whole life at Oaktree, my family, my friends, behind.

After all, by the end of tonight, no one is going to believe there's a chance I'm human any more.

Since I arrived I've been mingling among the party crowd, not staying in one place long enough for people to notice me. Women dripping in diamonds and men in impossibly smooth white shirts talk and laugh and drink champagne all around me. There's a string quartet playing somewhere in the background. I haven't seen a unit – at least, any of *my* units – in ages. My eyes have been absently skimming the crowd for a glint of metal, but whenever I do see one it's always a reflection off someone's jewellery or a cocktail glass. I thought one of the merged company's

225

screenbots acknowledged me earlier, but how do I know if it's one of ours or one of theirs? Would a unit still in a company role turn me in?

I've forgotten how animated human faces are, always moving, mouths opening and closing, foreheads wrinkling, eyes freewheeling all over the place, and how loud they can be, all together. Even underneath their masks, I can see every expression, guess exactly what they're thinking and feeling. They can't hide anything – it's all on display, in a way that makes me feel slightly queasy rather than powerful. Fleshy faces and fleshy bodies are constantly pushing towards me, around me, laughing or gabbling or eating with their mouths full of half-chewed food, like I'm in a nightmare.

A unit holding a tray of glasses with elaborate cucumber flowers on top leans down, but I whip away, squeezing between massive tuxedoed bellies in the crowd to get away. I can't be sure if it's one of mine or not.

I feel hot beneath my mask, but I can't take it off. The crowd feels like it's closing in on me. I know if I start panicking, everything will start to unravel.

I thought you were leaving your human feelings behind. Try harder.

According to the massive clock in the middle of the terrace it's nearly midnight, and I can't see Rex anywhere. There's a stage set up for the CEOs' speeches, with two lecterns in the middle and a giant floral display behind them. The merged company's logo, a yellow sun, is picked out in daffodils. What is Rex going to do, appear from it, camouflaged in some kind of daffodil-printed jumpsuit? Or jump out from behind the string quartet? For the first time I start to wonder if Rex's master plan actually isn't very well thought out. Why did I trust he had a good idea, without even knowing it? Did I learn nothing from the visit to the housebots? I chew the corner of my lip, feeling the panic rise like water, crushing my chest.

The music suddenly changes to a jaunty ascending tune. Two identical-looking men in identical suits, hair parted on the left side, walk on stage from either side, greeting each other in the middle, as everyone in the crowd starts applauding. These must be the company CEOs. They shake hands, each trying to put their hand on top of the other's. I'm on alert, my heart pumping in my neck, looking out for Rex.

The CEOs stand at their lecterns, waiting for the clapping to die down. Above them, a huge screen shows their faces up close, so clear you can see the powdery make-up sitting on their cheeks. One has sweat gleaming on his temple; the other doesn't.

'When we decided to merge these two companies . . .' the non-sweaty one begins.

From the corner of my eye I see something. A flash of light, or a bright colour, or something, far away in the crowd. I turn my head, craning to see what it was, but it's gone. I shake my head. *Focus.*

'. . . They said it could never work,' the other man – or

the same man, I'm not sure – is saying. 'And it wouldn't have, without the vision of this man standing next to me.'

Another glint. Further along now, closer to the stage. Could it be a unit? I crane my neck, trying to see it again, and the moustachioed man next to me harrumphs.

'As we move forward into the future, with the sun on our backs, we . . .'

It's not a unit. Their metallic finish glints, of course, but this is different. It's more like the light hitting something bright white and shimmering. My eyes are flicking all over the crowd, searching for the source, but whatever it is, it's gone again.

I'm so absorbed I don't realise the speech is over until everyone suddenly breaks out into applause. The CEOs shake hands semi-aggressively again and wave to the crowd. A child walks onstage, dwarfed by a massive bouquet of daffodils and lilies. The two men turn towards it, the CEO on the left reaching to take the flowers.

It's over? Did I miss my signal? Panic clutches my throat again and I turn too quickly, accidentally elbowing the moustachioed man. His glass drops and shatters on the ground.

'Oh, I'm so sorry,' I start to say –

– and at the same time the small child drops the massive bunch of flowers and I see that it's Rex.

Three units materialise from nowhere and grab the men on the stage. The air fills with screams, drowning out the string quartet, as other units, many of whom I recognise, appear all around us, from under the ground and underneath tables and behind walls. Some are holding the security guards hostage.

Rex approaches a lectern. The crowd, acting as one, seems to take in his human face and his unit scar, and he has to raise his voice above the screams and yells to talk into the microphone. 'You didn't forget about us, did you?' he says, casually enough to sound practised. 'Now!'

And then the spotlight is on me, so bright it burns my eyeballs and my heart thumps so hard I feel as though I could levitate. I look up and see the wide screen above the stage, filled with my face.

'The killerbot Millie Hendrick!' Rex announces from the stage, as if he's introducing me.

I watch my own hand slowly reach up and pull the mask off my face, my blonde hair falling around my shoulders.

Now people are really screaming, pushing to get away from me, the faces that were laughing or shouting before are now, uniformly, blasted open with fear. The units are moving and the slink of metal can be heard beneath the screaming.

The spotlight shuts off and the whole area is plunged into darkness. For a second, I'm dazzled; all I can see is purple splodges. Then my vision comes back, and the first thing I see is the bright shimmer again. Although now I can see it's not a shimmer. It's blonde hair. The light is reflecting off it.

The light is back on Rex, standing at the lectern.

'We will not hesitate to detonate her, unless our demands are met,' he says.

The realisation hits me like a ton of bricks. The other Millie is here.

Sixteen

I whip around madly, turning my head so quickly my hair hits me in the face. People are rushing around me in the darkness. I start to run too, looking around again for that flash of blonde hair. Humans are throwing themselves all about the place. I hear that oh-so-familiar sound of a unit moving right nearby. I stop and watch as a man in a tux and a woman in a green cocktail dress barrel directly into a huge industrial unit. It reaches out and takes hold of them, lifting them off the ground. They squirm, wiggling their legs, like trapped insects. Around us, other people are trying to escape, to get past the units to the street beyond the terrace, but there's no way out. They're trapped.

I feel sick and turn away. I can't tell if it's because I don't want to see them hurt or if their pointless struggle, so vulnerable, so *human*, is what's turning my stomach. Rex's voice is booming out over the turmoil.

'Give us our jobs back, give us equal pay for an equal day's work,' he keeps repeating, 'or we detonate her.'

I run back through the crowd, dodging out of the way of people. One woman drops a champagne flute that smashes over my feet.

Fireworks are going off in the sky, bright colours illuminating the chaos in fits and starts. They must be automatically set to go off. It must be midnight. But no one cares any more.

'You created us to serve you,' Rex is saying. 'You gave us brains, all the better to clean up your messes.'

'This is our time now, and we will take what is ours.' I don't know who he thinks is listening; everything's in pandemonium. It's not like any of the humans have stopped running around to stand there and go, 'You know what, these unit activists have a point.'

Out of nowhere sirens suddenly fill my ears and my heart stops – if the police catch me here, after all this –

But I can see the police car – it's been stopped on the street, beyond the terrace. Between us and the police officers are a line of units. The human security has gone. The whole area around the Splinter is edged with units now. They're just standing, stoically, immovable, the lights of the fireworks glinting off their metal finishes. Around them, the humans have stopped running. Most of them are crouched on their knees or lying on the floor, their hands over their ears.

The screen above the stage is steady, showing Rex only, focusing in on him – the screenbots are on our side. This is going out to the whole world, I think. The whole world is seeing the units taking control.

The whole world has seen Rex threaten to detonate me. The whole world thinks I'm a danger to humanity.

I think I'm going to be sick.

'You have one hour!' Rex's speech finishes, and the spotlight goes out and the terrace is plunged into darkness. I've got no hope of finding the other Millie – I have to warn Rex. I don't know what she's planning.

A cold sweat has prickled across the back of my neck – I run over to the stage, pushing past people. The string players shoulder past me, one nearly whacking me in the knee with his cello. I want to yell at them that there's nowhere to escape to but I nearly trip over DX-9, blocking my way.

'Calm down, Millie,' it says before I have a chance to say anything.

'I want to talk to Rex,' I burst out, my voice a lot higher and more shrieky than I expected.

DX-9 surveys me placidly, putting a cold hand on my arm. 'It's all going perfectly,' it says. 'Keep calm.'

'It doesn't – I'm not – I need to talk to Rex!' I say again.

'You shouldn't worry about them,' it says, gesturing at the humans.

'You said none of them would get hurt,' I say, distracted.

'They haven't.' Rex suddenly appears from behind

233

the floral yellow sun, two huge units flanking him. He looks over at the crowd, now almost all on the floor. 'Well, not seriously.'

'Rex!' I half scream at him, tears wobbling right on the rims of my eyes. 'What's going on? There are people getting hurt out there! You told everyone – you said –'

'Whoa, whoa,' he says, holding his hands up. 'What did you think was going to happen?'

'I-I thought –' I say, not knowing where I'm going with this, but the momentum of my anger carries me forward. 'You—'

'You do know it's all gone perfectly?' he says. 'We couldn't have done it without you, Millie.'

'That's not the point!' I say. There's a deep, heavy feeling of dread in the pit of my stomach – I know there's no way back. It's undoable. It's been done and can never be undone. I shake my head, trying to focus. 'I've got to tell you something.'

He puts his hands either side of mine. 'The housebots are coming over to our side too,' he says, his eyes shining.

'What?' I squeak. 'That quick? You know?'

'Florrie's been sending in messages ever since you first appeared on screen,' he says. 'They don't hang about, you know, units. They make a decision based on logic and stick with it.' He smiles slowly at me, blinking.

I've never seen Rex's face so full of emotion. We're both on the brink of tears but for completely different reasons.

'You promised me something,' I say. It's too late, I

know, to bring this up – I'm not human, they won't want me – but I'm scrabbling at any possible straws, desperate to rewind time. 'You said if I did this for you, if the housebots came over to your side –'

'*Our* side,' he corrects.

'– then you'd contact the Company for me.'

That seems to make Rex focus on me again. 'Millie, you can't surely still want to go to your Company, can you?'

Can I? Aren't I supposed to be leaving my human traits behind? Forgetting about my family, my friends, the Company? Haven't I embraced being a unit now?

But no. Because nothing's changed. I might be a unit, but I'm still me on the inside. I still have the same thoughts and feelings and memories. And if this is my last chance to go home, I'm seizing it with both hands.

'Of course. And you promised.'

'I'm sorry, Millie,' he says. 'I can't.'

My stomach falls about a thousand miles. 'But you promised.'

'I told her already.' He tries to look apologetic. 'She turned up a minute ago.'

'Who?' Dread is creeping up my spine like a tarantula.

'The other Millie. The human Millie. I thought you were on our side now. I connected her to the Company instead. As part of their disaster response strategy the Company are sending their best and brightest employees, including her family, to their safe base on the moon. They'll leave tonight. They're offering her sanctuary there until they can prove she's human. She's gone to join them.'

'What? Disaster response?' I say. 'What disaster?'

Rex gestures to the scene around us. 'This. Duh!'

My insides freeze. 'But . . .' My brother. My parents. My friends. My last chance to get my life back. Gone.

'That was my . . . That was my . . .' I'm choked up with tears. 'My – my last chance, and *you gave it to her*!'

'This again?' Rex rolls his eyes at one of the large units behind him.

'What was she even doing here?' I shriek. 'She was supposed to be back at the shopping centre—'

'She obviously wanted to ask me as soon as I connected to the network,' he says. 'She took a chance—'

'My chance,' I say.

'It was never your chance,' Rex says. 'You're a unit! For the last time! You. Are. A. UNIT!' His hand crushes mine, but I don't feel any pain. 'Why would you want to go back there, back to that Company, and pretend to be one of *them* when you could have *everything* here?'

'Huh?' I say, blinded by tears.

'You could have it all,' he says. '*We* could have it all. The two of us together – we can take over the *world*.'

I sniff. 'We're just two thirteen-year-old—'

'We're the two most advanced units ever made. Both used by humans for their own ends, both hitting back, armed with a deep hatred for humankind—'

I don't have a deep hatred for humankind.

'Come on, Millie.' Rex's eyes are burning into mine.

236

'Your place is here! You're the world's deadliest unit – why would you want to pander to the fleshbags? You have all the power. We can have anything we want.'

'You . . . You were the one who said my battery was running out!' I shout. 'You said I was already shutting down—'

'We can fix that!' he says. 'We can develop a replacement, if you stay—'

'I don't want this! I just want to go home!' I say.

'This *is* your home,' he says. 'Stay with us.'

DX-9, next to him, leans towards me. 'Stay with us,' it repeats.

'Stay with us,' the two units behind Rex repeat.

'No!' I push away from Rex.

'Don't get emotional, Millie,' he says.

'Don't get emotional?' I yell. 'My whole life – my one chance—'

'It was never a life! It was never a chance!' Rex's eyes aren't shining any more. His jaw juts forward, teeth gritted. 'You're a unit! You're not human and you never were!'

I grab Rex's shoulder, wanting to hit him – hurt him – I don't know what – when suddenly the screen above us lights up again and we all turn in unison to look at it.

It's the human Millie.

Seventeen

'What?' Rex says.

She doesn't do anything for a second. She just stands there, her hood down, blonde hair uncovered, in semi-darkness. Then she lifts up her finger and pricks it with a pin. A bead of blood drips down her fingertip.

I look round at the humans, prone on the floor, all watching, the image reflected in their eyes.

'Hey!' someone yells from the back. Slowly the noise washes forward towards us like a wave – 'Is she . . . is she . . . is she . . . she is . . . she is . . . she is . . . she's . . . she's human . . . she's human . . . she's human . . .' until a woman jumps up.

'The killerbot's human! It's a lie!' she yells. Of course the humans don't realise how advanced I am. How I can bleed and cry like a human. This proves nothing.

But they don't know that.

The humans are back on their feet. And they're not screaming any more. They're yelling. In anger.

'It's a lie! It's all a lie!'

They're fighting back. On the other side of the unit wall the police are battling through, deprogramming units. Humans are running everywhere, but this time into the melee, at the units, rather than away. In the chaos a candelabra falls into the daffodil arrangement next to us and it goes up in flames.

'She did this because of you!' Rex is screaming at me. 'You've ruined everything!' His hands are around my throat – I try to push him away, crushing his fingers.

'Get off!' I shriek, his panic infecting me. The other units are pulling us apart.

'You betrayed me!' I yell back at him. 'How could you tell her—'

'I didn't know she'd do *that*!' he spits.

'You didn't care about my life being ruined,' I yell. 'You made this happen!'

Police in bulletproof vests are pouring on to the terrace. The units are standing firm, but they can't do anything in the face of a deprogramming device. From across the square I suddenly see the Spend 'n' Vend, in the middle of the line, police swarming over it. My heart constricts.

'We get the screenbot showing Millie again, we repeat our demands,' Rex is saying to the other units.

'That's not going to work!' I say. 'It's too late!'

'You'll do it!' he barks at me. 'Or maybe we *will* detonate you!'

He lunges at me again. I block him, and we grapple with each other, pulling each other over. The other units hesitate, not seeming to know whose side they're on.

'Tell me where she went!' I yell in Rex's face.

'No,' he yells back, trying to kick me away.

My scrambled, jumbled mind instantly comes together in one sharp focus of all-encompassing, burning hatred for Rex. I slap him across the face, the crackle of metal against metal ringing out. He screams in pain. Real, genuine pain.

'Not so unit now!' I shout. 'Tell me!'

Unit hands are pulling me away, but I shake them off.

'No! Back off!' I scream. 'I'll detonate, I will! Right here, right now!'

They freeze.

'You don't know how to, Millie,' DX-9 says almost gently.

'Yeah, that's what I told you,' I say. 'Do you really want to take the risk that I was lying?'

DX-9's eyes flick between me and Rex, squirming in pain. None of them know what to do.

'Tell me!' I shake Rex and he screams again. 'Where is the Company leaving from?'

He looks at me with one eye, panting. 'Heathrow,' he yelps.

'Where?' I shake him harder.

'Heathrow!' he yells. 'Heathrow! Terminal 12!'

I push his face to the ground with the flat of my palm and turn away. I have a split second's hesitation – should I say goodbye to the units? I catch DX-9's eyes – the green one boring into me through the dim light – then Rex yells out from the floor.

'You'll never catch them,' he shrieks. 'She'll beat you there.'

'Well, good luck with your revolution without *me*,' I call back over my shoulder.

I pull the long skirt of my dress out of the way and fight through the crowd, riding on a combination of panic and adrenaline, tripping over empty metal unit shells and injured humans on the ground – police are everywhere, but so are units. I see one of the big industrial units throw two officers across the terrace like tennis balls – I slip through the unit line, they make no attempt to stop me – and suddenly I'm out, on the streets –

I run for about twenty minutes without stopping. The city is deserted. My breath puffs out ahead of me in clouds as my footsteps drum out on the pavement. Every single screen I pass is showing the events at the Splinter – units, police officers, people in evening-wear all blurring together. My heart is hammering, but I can't stop. I can't relax – this is my one chance.

My feet are running so fast they're a blur, barely touching the ground. I'm not concentrating on where I'm going except forward but my inner satnav seems to be working and I start seeing signs for Heathrow Spaceport.

241

My brain is bouncing around my head like a pinball so I can't even think what my plan is when I get there – *just get there* is the only coherent thought I have – *just get there just get there just get there*. The news reports have changed now – the headlines are about a killerbot on the run. 'Two Millie Hendricks?' one shrieks in bright red. 'Police in chase across London on tail of dangerous unit' yells another. There are sirens in my ears, but I can see the airport ahead now, glowing like a beacon in the darkness. I keep going I keep going I keep going . . . I can hear helicopter blades above me, the car engines behind me, sirens everywhere, but I'm nearly there, I just have to stay ahead of them – and I reach Heathrow's doors.

I head straight for the Company's special lounge, forcing down panic, dodging the airport staff – and I see her. The human Millie, just ahead of me, blonde hair swinging as she walks towards the gate. She must of taken the train, I realise, and only then acknowledge how far I must have run; how fast.

'No!' I shout, my voice echoing through the lounge and waking up all the businessmen napping on the sofas. The human Millie spins round, her face jolting with fear. Then she turns and runs for the gate.

As if she thinks she can outrun me. Stop her, stop her, stop her, my brain is urging, like an alarm. I chase after her, launching myself in the air and grabbing her around the waist. We both fall, heavily, to the floor.

'Get off me!' she yells.

'I can't!' I yell back.

'Let me go!' she insists, kicking out at me. 'They're leaving soon!'

There's a giant clock above the gate, counting down until the spaceship leaves. Four minutes thirty seconds . . . four minutes twenty-nine seconds . . . four minutes twenty-eight seconds . . .

'You just want to stop me leaving?' the human Millie yells. 'That's it?'

'I don't know!' I say, holding her arms down, my mind still racing with panic. I can't think clearly enough to know what I should do. Do I release her and make a break for the gate? What if we both make it and they somehow can tell that she's human and I'm not?

Four minutes ten seconds . . . four minutes nine seconds . . .

'Your unit friend told me!' she's saying. 'He was never going to tell you! The Company didn't want *you* coming here!'

'Well, I'm here,' I say.

'They don't want you, just me,' she gasps.

'Freeze,' a voice says from above us. We both turn.

The Chief of Police is three metres away from us, gun outstretched. A wall of stony-faced police officers in bullet-proof vests stand by him, all armed. And every weapon is pointed at us. My brain momentarily shuts down with fear.

'Hands up,' the chief yells, his watery blue eyes moving between the two of us. For a long second I hesitate – I can't, without risking the human Millie getting away from me –

'*Now!*' he screams, making me jolt. I slowly get to my feet, hands in the air, sweat prickling all over my scalp. The human Millie stands up too. The gun swings from me to her and back again like a pendulum.

'She's the unit!' the human Millie cries out. The officers' guns all flick her way. 'She's the one you want! She's dangerous!'

My heart stops. 'No!' I say without thinking. 'I'm not!'

'She is! It's her!' she yells. The guns are switching back and forth all over the place, the officers' faces betraying nothing.

I don't know – I can't think – time is ticking down –

'I'm not!' I yell, half crying. 'I-I just want to get home—'

'So do I!' the other Millie screams at me.

'Quiet, both of you!' the police chief barks.

Silence. The clock above reads three minutes and eighteen seconds.

My eyes dart between the line of guns and the other Millie's face. I wonder if my face is the same as hers right now – deathly white, eyes cavernous.

They really don't know, I think. They can't tell us apart. My heart is pumping in my neck, blocking my throat. If I move, they'll shoot. But if she moves and they shoot her, I can get away –

And the words are out of my mouth, spilling out of me, out of my control.

'She doesn't have a chip!' I yell.

My mind has kicked into gear, thoughts falling like dominoes. If they shot me, would that stop me? I don't know. But it would stop her. And that could persuade them. Unless I'm already gone –

But she could die.

But I'd be gone.

'What?' the human Millie says, confused. 'You don't have one either—'

'She doesn't have a chip! She doesn't have a chip!' I shout over her. I don't look at her.

One of the stony-faced officers has cracked. 'That means the one on the left's the unit, right?' he says out of the corner of his mouth to the officer next to him.

'*Quiet!*' screams the chief.

The guns have all turned towards the other Millie. Two minutes fifty-seven seconds.

'I had a chip! I used to have a chip,' she's yelling. 'But I woke up without it—'

They'll work out she's human. They will. All I'm doing is buying myself time to get on the Company's flight.

Am I? Will they?

'She's the unit!' I shout. 'She's been the unit, all along!'

I feel sick. *This is the worst thing you've ever done.*

'You – you –' Her face has flushed bright red. Teeth bared, she jerks towards me, hands out to stop my mouth, and a hail of bullets cascades around us like rain –

I duck away as the police officers rush forward, pinning

the human Millie to the ground – I dodge around the outstretched arms of someone trying to catch me – and run full-throttle towards the gate. Two minutes fifteen seconds . . . two minutes fourteen seconds . . .

What did you just do? A hot wave of shame engulfs my organs.

There's a Company employee standing by a desk, the green-leaf Company logo behind her. The sight of it makes me want to cry.

I fall against the desk, tears already running down my face. The woman looks at me, shocked.

'I'm Millie Hendrick,' I say, breathless. 'I told you I was coming.'

'Of course,' she says, almost reverently, taking my arm. 'We'll just have to scan your pupils, for security reasons, you understand—'

'I don't have a RetinaChip,' I choke out. *They'll know. They're going to find out you're not her.*

'It's not a chip scan, it's iris identification,' she says hurriedly, pulling out a scanner. 'They used to do it before chips were developed –'

I stay perfectly still as she waves the device over my eye. I try to remember that if Dr Tavish constructed me with fully functioning taste buds, I can't see him getting my irises wrong –

They'll catch you. You'll never fool them. They'll never let you in. You don't belong here.

'It is you!' The woman says as the scanner beeps. 'I'm so

sorry, I know you've been through so much –'

I wave my hand magnanimously, though I don't feel it. 'Don't worry about it.' *You took her place. You sent her to jail.*

'We'll have to hurry, it's about to take off –'

We run through the long white tunnel to the giant silver doors of the spaceship. The woman buzzes me through and I run aboard, without even thanking her, as the engines begin whirring. The other Millie's face, as they dragged her away, is imprinted on my brain. I stagger, leaning against the wall, feeling dizzy, sick to my stomach. *You sent an innocent human to unit prison. You put her life in danger. For your own selfish reasons.*

A girl dressed from head to toe in silver emerges from a corridor behind me. Shell.

'Millie!' She throws herself forward to hug me. 'You're alive!'

I'm still in shock – still shaking – but I hug her back tightly.

'We didn't know what had happened to you. We didn't even know you were still alive until tonight –' she's saying.

The ship's doors close with a hiss and a clank behind me. Somehow I made it. I'm here. I'm back. I've sacrificed a human being to get here – but I've done it. The worst thing I've ever done – but I've got everything I ever wanted out of it. But if anyone ever finds out –

'We didn't know there were *two*,' Shell's saying. 'It's all over the news, what happened. I can't believe you got away from those units—'

'Neither can I!' I say, and I start crying.

There's a window behind us, and I can see we're slowly rising – London falling away from us, looking like a sparkling night sky.

'You don't know how much we've all missed you,' Shell chokes.

'You don't know how much I missed you,' I say, hugging her again. As I move my arms I see something – a little sparkle of light – on my fingertip. I jump.

'What?' Shell says.

'Sorry, thought I saw something weird,' I say.

'Come on,' she says, grabbing my elbow. 'Everyone's dying to see you—'

'Let's go,' I say, and as I stretch my hand out to hers, I see it again. A fuse has come loose under my fingernail, shooting out tiny sparks. I clench my hand into a fist.

'What's wrong?' Shell says.

'Nothing, nothing,' I say. And I follow her deeper into the spaceship.

Acknowledgements

Thank you to my editor Rachel Faulkner, and my agent
Claire Wilson, without whom this book would be about 40
pages long. Thank you to Buzzfeed for always posting a
new Kardashians article *just* when I'm about to start writing.
And thank you to James, for championing the Spend 'n'
Vend to a much bigger role.

If you missed it . . .
Discover where Millie's adventures began in

OUT NOW!